£4.25

WHERE'S THAT?

The approximate locations of our picture features

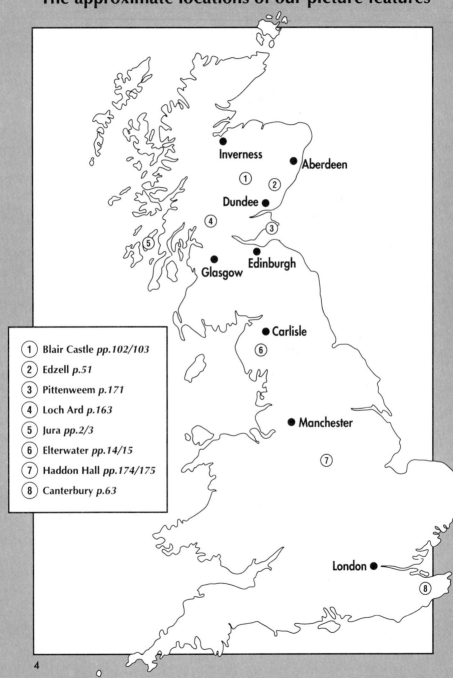

① Blair Castle *pp.102/103*

② Edzell *p.51*

③ Pittenweem *p.171*

④ Loch Ard *p.163*

⑤ Jura *pp.2/3*

⑥ Elterwater *pp.14/15*

⑦ Haddon Hall *pp.174/175*

⑧ Canterbury *p.63*

People's Friend Annual 1997

Contents

BACK COVER *Loch Awe from Ben Cruachan.*

He always says that if I hadn't kept a diary when I was seventeen, I wouldn't have remembered the way we first met. It isn't true — maybe it did go out of my head for years, but as soon as I saw him again it came back. Vividly.

Tonight I'm having the traditional bride's early night before the wedding tomorow, on the theory, I suppose, that then I'll drift up the aisle looking perfect and unlined and unworried.

Meanwhile, he'll be out on his stag night. I know he's bound to have his best mate as best man, but all things considered . . . Please could someone, somewhere, keep an eye on them?

I did tell him once that the wisest thing he could do was marry a doctor, but that was really a way of getting him to propose. All the same, I'd rather not spend my wedding-day on damage repairs . . .

That summer when I was seventeen, I was really rather plain (I remember only too well) and still suffering from puppy-fat. I was bookish and clever, too, using my clever-girl's sharp tongue as a defence — not like my cousin, Michelle, with whom I'd been sent to stay for part of the summer holidays.

Michelle and I were the same age but she was one of those miraculous early bloomers — a perfect, slender figure, long, shining, blonde hair, flawless skin, big blue eyes.

I always thought she didn't have two brain cells to rub together, though that was probably envy. Actually, I still don't think she has, but she's very sweet natured. We really didn't have much in common, and still don't.

Be that as it may, I'd been sent off to stay with her so that we could be "company for each other." That part of the family

Accident Prone!

by FRANCES FERGUSON

live near Rye. It's pretty there — the river, the sea not far away, an attractive countryside full of old villages and farms.

Michelle was mad about a boy called Andrew Whitaker. It was just about the first thing she told me when I arrived — how handsome he was, how athletic, how brilliant, etcetera, etcetera. He was nineteen and had just started studying to be an accountant.

I bet he's a drag, I thought nastily, as I heard how everyone, but everyone, was dying for him to ask them out.

And wasn't it absolutely *brilliant*, Michelle said with her eyes sparkling, after a couple of days of this: Andrew had invited both of us to spend the day with him and a friend of his on a boat, on the river.

He and Joe (the friend) had promised to do some small repair to

Joe's uncle's cabin cruiser, and then after that we'd take the boat down the river for a lovely romantic day.

Andrew *was* handsome, I suppose. Like Michelle, he had escaped from, or already come out of, the twin teenage curses of lumpiness and acne.

He had shining, combed-back, dark hair, a straight profile, serious brown eyes, long, well-muscled brown legs under tidy shorts. He shook me gravely by the hand when I was introduced to him.

"This is my cousin Lucy, Lucy Graham," Michelle said.

Then he introduced me with equal gravity to the fourth member of the party, his friend Joe McCallum.

Joe and I, I thought tartly, (I said I was sharp-tongued, didn't I?) were the two inevitable plain friends of the two beautiful ones. Mind you, Joe wasn't spotty, either, just tall and skinny with a square jaw, a big wide grin, tufty hair, and sticking-out ears. He wrung my hand painfully after wiping his on the back of his cut-off jeans.

Once my uncle, who had driven us down to join the boys on the boat, went away after telling us all to take care of ourselves, we could start getting on with this minor repair the boys had promised to perform before we took properly to the water.

"What we've got to do," Joe said enthusiastically, "is drill down into the bilges and fit a small pump. Shouldn't take long!

"Um — I reckon the girls had better sit up on top while we're doing it. Don't you think so, Andy? I mean, you might get dirty down here with us!"

There was a spell of giggling from Michelle while she got Andrew to lift her on to the cabin cruiser's roof. I scrambled up perfectly well by myself. Then we were supposed to sit there and look admiring while the he-men did their clever mechanical stuff.

I'd brought a book in with our picnic things — just so I could bury my head in it and show how boring everything was, if I wanted to.

Actually, it was rather a nice cabin cruiser, about twenty feet long, white and sleek. The river was wide and full just here, winding its reed-fringed way through the flat land, and the sun was shining.

There should have been worse things to do than sunbathe on the cabin roof while the boys leapt about in the well deciding on the right place to make a hole and plugging the drill in to the engine and doing a lot of efficient, masculine things.

It was Joe who was doing most of the leaping about and saying, "Hold that — no, let's put it there — don't switch on until I tell you — got it?"

And it was Andrew who glanced up at us apologetically when the tearing sound of the drill spoiled the quiet lap of water against the hull.

R IGHT, we're through, look — oh! Hang on a minute! Andy, we didn't — um — we didn't check where the bilges actually ended, did we? I think we might have missed them. I think —"

"I think you've gone right through the bottom of the boat," I said tartly from up above — stating the obvious, as a steady bubble of river water started to seep noticeably into the floor of the well.

"Yes, you're right," Joe said seriously, staring at his handiwork. Michelle let out a little shriek, and at once he was all cheerful consolation. "It's all right, I'll put something in it. We won't sink! Andy, shove your finger in there for a minute while I find something to bung it with!"

He disappeared into the cabin while Andrew obediently thrust one finger into the hole. It did stop the water, but left him rather tied down.

You couldn't fault Joe. He might drill holes in the bottom of boats by mistake, but he believed in putting his mistakes right.

A moment later he'd reappeared triumphantly with a short length of dowelling. Then there was the business of cutting it down, sanding it, making sure it would fit . . .

Michelle leaned down to make fluttery but encouraging comments, and Andrew tried to answer her without stopping his boy-with-a-finger-in-the-dyke exercise. At last the bung was triumphantly in place, and working, and the boys stood up looking a lot grubbier than they had been when they started.

"OK! Sorry about that," Joe apologised. "I don't think we'd better drill again until I'm sure where the bilges actually are. Tell you what, we're riverworthy now so let's just go on as we planned. We can take the boat right out of the water when we get to the slipway at the other end, and do the repair later!"

THEY started the engine and cast off. We were a little way down river, right in the middle — with Michelle at the wheel learning how to steer — when the bung flew out under the pressure of water, and somehow disappeared.

Joe didn't panic. We had a spell with Andrew's finger in the hole again while Joe looked for something else to use.

There wasn't any more dowelling, but eventually they settled on Andrew's pen-top. Miraculously, it not only filled the hole exactly, but even looked as if it would stay there.

"I should think you girls must be getting a bit hungry, aren't you?" Joe was being thoughtful again. "Time's getting on a bit, so let's eat as we go along. Oh!"

Our new, smooth progress came to a sudden juddering halt.

The river at Rye is tidal. I'd thought it looked narrower and with wider edges as we came round the last bend. Now, even though we were in the middle, it seemed we'd hit a mud-flat.

Before we could back off it, the engine gave a cough, and died.

The boys looked at each other and you could see them thinking, all of a sudden, that they'd forgotten to check how much petrol there was in the tank. Sure enough, the gauge showed empty.

"There's bound to be a spare can on board somewhere!" Joe said with undying optimism, and went to hunt for it.

He came back empty-handed, and ran one grubby hand through his

THE FARMER AND HIS WIFE

ANNE says that second-hand bookshops, butchers and greengrocers are all magnets to me. That's like the pot calling the kettle black — she loves wandering round antique shops.

I went into a second-hand bookshop in St Andrews and saw an illustrated book entitled "Pressure Cooking," price originally £1 reduced to 25p. It was beautifully illustrated, and the photos of the cooked meals made my mouth water.

I remembered that years back, I bought Anne a pressure cooker. We tried it once! We were both scared stiff, and put it in the dairy where it has sat on a shelf ever since.

I bought that book but didn't then show it to Anne.

I pondered.

Who in the farming fraternity had a pressure cooker? Whom dare I ask to show us how to use it without blowing ourselves up? And what's more important, not let on I'd asked?

I was in Cupar one Tuesday when I saw Molly approaching. We chatted and I casually asked, "Molly, have you a pressure cooker?"

"Wouldn't be without it, John."

I explained about the book and our ancient cooker and how I would like Anne to learn how to use it.

"Easy, John, leave it to me."

ABOUT a week later I came in for my breakfast.

"John, Molly wants us to go for a meal next Friday night."

I smiled to myself. Good old Molly.

Molly excelled herself. It was a cold night and for the first course she had made carrot and orange soup, followed by casserole of pork chops and then, to crown the meal, honey and lemon sponge with lashings of home-made custard.

tufty hair, looking sheepish and apologetic.

"Oh, Andrew, what are we going to do?" Michelle wailed, fluttering her eyelashes at him.

"Er — well, I suppose we'll have to wait for another boat to come upriver and hope they've got a spare can." Joe advised with undimmed cheerfulness. "The tide's going out all the time, so we shouldn't risk it!

"What we'll do is, I'll take a line and tow us by swimming. These Fibre-glass hulls aren't all that heavy . . ."

He leapt heroically over the side — and landed, looking very surprised, in water which came no farther than his knees.

Even that didn't defeat him. He'd soon organised things so that Andrew would steer, and he'd tow — walking.

(I did offer, impatiently, to get over into the mud with him, but he wouldn't let me. Michelle didn't even offer.)

Joe must have been stronger than his skinny frame looked, because we did move. He was amazingly cheerful about the whole thing, even when he took a step and suddenly disappeared, because we'd hit a

10

by
John
Taylor

Anne was really impressed.

"Molly, I don't know how you do it," she complimented our hostess.

"Simple, all done in no time in the pressure cooker," Molly explained.

After the meal, whilst Alistair and I were washing up, Anne was given lessons on how to use this steaming monster.

Next day, when I came in for breakfast, I smiled — Anne was really giving our old pressure cooker the clean of its life.

I took off my wellingtons, went to my desk and I handed her my 25p book of recipes.

"When did you buy this, John?"

"About a month ago."

There was a pause when she gave me an old-fashioned look, then she said accusingly, "John, did you put Molly up to giving us that meal?"

I said, with as straight a face as I could manage, "Oh, no, dear, I would never have done that."

I don't think she believed me!

WHEN I came in for lunch, I was relieved to see Anne was all smiles. I thought she might have been cross, very cross.

"John, you're a liar," she declared.

Anne had been on the phone to Molly to thank her for the beautiful meal, and had wormed out of her about meeting me in Cupar and how could I get Anne to use the pressure cooker. She had even repeated her parting shot — "Easy, John, leave it to me."

I noted that on the table was my 25p book.

"I'm going to make lamb, potato and leek soup, John," Ann declared.

Yes, we had soup for our late tea which is also supper, our last meal of the day. It was really beautiful, and Anne was like a cat with two tails because she'd made it in the pressure cooker!

channel where the water was deeper.

Just as we were floating again, another boat did come upriver, and offered us a tow down through the channels, too.

Joe came back on board, grinning, and shook himself enthusiastically, which spattered all of us with river mud, before he took over the steering.

We hadn't gone far before the pen-top sprang out of the bung-hole, to vanish just as the first bung had done. No amount of scrabbling about in the well discovered it.

There was only one thing for it — Andrew, since Joe was steering, stuck his finger in place again.

We got to the other end and, with help, drew the boat up on the slipway.

Then we found out that Andrew's finger was stuck. He'd pushed it in too far against the rough edges of the Fibre-glass, and trying to pull it out only made it swell.

Joe was restrained from hauling on him helpfully and, (since the boat was out of the water now), someone had to come with a power-saw and cut a larger, tidy hole.

Michelle was busy having hysterics in case his finger got cut off entirely, and Joe was trying to comfort her. I was the one who held things still and encouraged Andrew not to flinch at the wrong moment. Well, I *was* already planning to go to medical school, so you could say it was all practice.

He went off to hospital after that, to have the rest of the Fibre-glass taken off, and his finger X-rayed.

Somehow he didn't seem keen on taking Michelle out again during those holidays. Luckily she'd stopped being all that keen either.

"Andrew's wonderful, but he's always with that Joe McCallum," she said crossly, "and when they're both there it's like — like —"

"Like trying to co-exist with an over-enthusiastic Old English Sheepdog puppy?" I suggested tartly.

"I mean, everyone always says Joe's very nice natured, but it would be easier if — they're just so inseparable, and it never seems to occur to Andrew that it might be more fun to be alone . . ."

MY holiday finished. I went home, then back to school, to take my final exams, then to university and medical school.

Michelle trained to be a dancer, got engaged three times in quick succession, finally married an Italian and settled down in Milan to have several children.

It was eight years before I saw Andrew Whitaker and Joe McCallum again.

When I landed up at the foot of Andrew's hospital bed in my white coat he didn't recognise me. Well, I'd fined down a lot (one does, on hospital hours) and my hair was different, short and sleek which suits me better. Once my face had thinned and my cheek-bones had the chance to show, I was really quite a lot better looking.

Anyway, even though I was back in the Rye area, he probably wasn't expecting to see me as Dr Lucy Graham, orthopaedic house-surgeon.

I recognised *him,* though, even lying flat on his back with his leg in plaster and raised in traction. He wasn't quite as smoothly handsome as he'd been at nineteen, but he was still very good looking.

I recognised the visitor sitting beside his bed, too. Joe McCallum hadn't changed much, except to fill out a bit round the shoulders. He was still tall and skinny, square-jawed, tufty-haired, and with an air of undaunted cheerfulness. Besides, you couldn't miss those sticking-out ears.

Surprisingly, he knew who I was, too (I found out later that he'd kept up with Michelle's parents), and he gave me a shy grin and asked how I was.

"I'm fine, thanks, but I need to examine this new patient of mine who seems to have come in during my night off. So if you wouldn't mind leaving us to it for a few minutes —?"

He gave me another shy grin and got up. As I drew the curtains round Andrew's bed, I saw him moving up the ward to chat to one of the old men who hadn't got any visitors.

I looked at Andrew's notes. "I see you broke your leg falling off a farm cottage roof. Funny place for an accountant. What were you trying to do up there?"

"Joe offered to unblock the chimney so the farmer could re-let the cottage," he explained. "I said I'd help out, but I slipped."

I checked him over quickly. He seemed to be all right except for the nasty break in his leg.

"You've got quite a lot of notes here, going back over the years," I remarked. "You broke your arm taking some children on a merry-go-round? You came in covered with wasp stings after trying to help shift a nest? You cut your leg when a power-saw slipped? You've been in and out of out-patients with concussion a couple of times, too.

"You do seem to be one of the hospital's more regular patients! Have you ever thought of spending your spare time in some less dangerous way — like, say, hang-gliding?" (Yes, I know, I was still pretty sharp-tongued.)

As he looked at me sheepishly, I added, "Tell me, though I bet I can guess — was your friend Joe with you on all those occasions?"

"You can't blame Joe!" Andrew protested. "When I fell off the roof we were miles from anywhere, and he carried me on his back all the way to the farmhouse to get to a phone!"

"Really? Then you're lucky your leg isn't worse than it is!" I retorted, swishing the curtains back from round him. "Try to keep still — and *don't* let him touch your tractions!"

I SAW quite a lot of both of them after that — Andrew, because his leg was slow to heal, and Joe because he was in and out all the time as a visitor. Somehow I went on seeing both of them after Andrew was discharged, too.

They were still best mates, even after all these years, turning up in the same places, doing the same things — almost always helpful schemes of Joe's. Joe led and Andrew followed.

Andrew was a nice, conventional, successful accountant by now, with a good practice. Meanwhile Joe had done various things over the years, including being a motor-bike despatch-rider, a milkman, a helper in an old people's home, and then eventually he'd trained as a Youth and Community worker.

It seemed like a suitable place for his endless energy and enthusiasm, and he was good at it. I got drawn into their lives partly, I suppose, because I had some idea that if I was there I could put a sensible brake on things, and stop the worse disasters happening.

So that was how I came to be lying here with my fingers crossed about the stag night, hoping my tomorrow's bridegroom and his best man are going to be in church tomorrow in one piece.

There's a rattle of gravel against my open window. I rush over to it straight away and lean out.

The familiar, upturned face of my beloved is down there in the

ELTERWATER, CUMBRIA : J CAMPBELL KERR

garden in the bright moonlight.

"What are you doing here? Is everything all right —?"

"Yes, don't flap!" he assures me. "They're all sinking so many beers I don't suppose they'll miss me, and I don't want to be hungover tomorrow — it's too important. So I slipped away — I just wanted to see you . . ."

"You're a romantic at heart, aren't you?" I look down at him lovingly. "I do love you, Joe. You knew I'd be worrying, didn't you?"

"I'll be there on time at the church," he promises. "I won't be in some Casualty department trying to get Andy patched up. I've got a couple of the others to make sure he doesn't walk under a car on the way out of the pub.

"I must be the only bridegroom who has to worry about getting his best man there instead of the other way round."

Joe grins up at me, but there's something half serious in his eyes, too. "You know, I thought for ages it was him you were interested in, not me. I still find it hard to believe. I mean, it would have made sense — he's better looking, and more successful, and he's —"

"Much too biddable. I'd have ended up bossing him about, wouldn't I? Whereas you —" I look down at him. Joe's got no conceit at all, just a lot of enthusiasm, tremendous loyalty, and the sort of kindness which is like a warm place in a cynical world.

"Andy's very nice, but he's not you. What are you doing —?" I ask in alarm.

L OOKING for a drain-pipe to climb," my beloved says determinedly, scrabbling about amongst the creeper on the wall below my bedroom window. "Romeo managed to shin up to Juliet's balcony, didn't he? So —"

"Don't! With your luck it'll come away from the wall and then you'll insist on spending half the night trying to repair it!" I warn him.

Joe steps back.

"Oh, well, I suppose I'll have to wait until tomorrow to kiss you," he grumbles, but looking up at me with his wide grin, and a blaze of

◀ p15.

ELTERWATER, CUMBRIA.

A SMALL lake, Elterwater is just north of Windermere at the entrance to Great Langdale and Little Langdale with crags beloved of climbers. Near Elterwater village, at St Martin's Farm, John Ruskin, the 19th-century philanthropist, established a centre for a revival of the hand-made linen industry.

love in his face. "I just came to say goodnight — and, you will, really, come up that aisle in the morning, won't you?"

"Oh, I'll be there. I wouldn't miss it. And to make sure you don't, will you *please* go back to your hotel room now, and go to sleep?"

"All right. Goodnight, love. See you in church . . ."

We blow each other kisses. He pretends to catch mine and swallow them. Then he's fading back into the garden, and I'm waving, and he's waving, and then he's gone.

It's ten years since I first met him, and thought he was a pain and his best friend was handsome but wet. (Actually I'm still tempted to think that about Andy, but I wouldn't tell Joe so.)

It's funny how your view of people changes. Being with Joe can still sometimes be exasperating, and like co-existing with an over-enthusiastic Old English Sheepdog puppy. But I love him, and life with him will never be dull.

Maybe we can find a nice quiet Casualty nurse to marry Andy off to — to save me having to spend the next goodness-knows-how-many years patching up my husband's accident-prone best friend! □

The Patchwork of Friendships

*F*RIENDSHIPS *vary, each unique,*
    Patterned deeply, or pastel
    sweet . . .
Friendships near, we often seek,
Some dark, intense, remain
    discreet . . .
Like patchwork fields around a farm.

Some run quickly to a peak,
Then drop to shadow, sink in
    peat . . .
Like patchwork fields around a farm.

Friendships tried, care-ridged, not
    sleek,
Sun-kissed and cheering as we
    greet . . .
Like patchwork fields around a farm.

Best are those as strong as teak,
Yet, all are welcomed, and complete
My vibrant pastures, treasured, warm.

— *Anna Cole.*

B

With A Little Help From Gran....

IT was all right for Lucy, James thought miserably. She was only three. It was easy for her to like Matthew, because she'd never known anyone else. She had no idea how things used to be. And she'd never made promises she might not be able to keep . . .

It wasn't that James didn't like Matthew. Matthew was fun and he'd made them all happy again. But James had made a special promise to his dad.

"Look after your mum and sister," Dad had said, before he went away and never came back . . .

They'd said it was an accident. James knew about accidents — he'd seen them on television — but he'd never realised how awful they were.

Mum had tried to be normal for them, but James had seen how hard it was for her. He'd had to look after her then, all right. He'd really had to keep his promise . . .

He'd envied Lucy then. She was only eleven months old and had no idea what was happening. And, in a way, she'd got them all through it, for she'd still needed to be fed and cared for. And, in time, she'd learned to walk, and talk and, slowly, the world had returned to a kind of normal.

"Do I look after you, Mum?" he'd asked once, anxiously. "Dad told me to look after you and Lucy. Do I?"

"You're a treasure, James," his mum had said gently. "I

by SALLY BRAY

don't know what I'd do without you. I don't know what any of us would do without each other."

And then Mum met Matthew.

James hadn't minded at first. Matthew had just been a friend, someone she worked with, who'd brought her home when her car broke down. He'd chatted to James and been nice to Lucy, and Mum had smiled a lot and then asked him to tea.

Later, he'd mended James' Action Man and told him all about the toys he'd had when *he* was young, and it had been almost like talking to Dad again.

And after that, they'd seen Matthew constantly. He'd come to tea, he'd taken them out, he'd invited them round to visit him. In no time at all he was part of their lives. And then Mum had said they were going to get married . . .

"Is that all right, love?" she'd asked anxiously. "You don't mind, do you?"

Married. He'd never once thought they might get married . . .

19

JAMES was rather quiet for the next few days, but no-one noticed; after all, he was often quiet.

Then, on Sunday, Matt announced he was taking them out for a picnic. James immediately asked if he could stay behind.

"I've said I'll go and play with Robin," he said. "We're making a dinosaur park." It wasn't true, but he didn't want to go out with them, not today. He wanted to be alone.

"You never said anything about it before," his mother pointed out, and James blushed.

"I forgot," he mumbled, but to his relief his mother only laughed.

"Getting absent-minded in your old age?" she asked affectionately. "OK, then, if that's what you want. We'll drop you off on the way."

James hadn't bargained for that, but he couldn't argue. Within minutes he was being piled into the car with everyone else and driven to his friend's house.

Lucy was singing loudly and tunelessly in her safety seat and Matt and Mum were cracking jokes. It was all very hectic and for the first time it got on his nerves. But at last they reached Robin's house.

To keep up the pretence he walked down the drive. The car seemed to wait beside the kerb for a horribly long time.

Moving into the shadow of the house he hid among the bushes, willing his mother and Matt to leave. By some miracle none of Robin's family saw him.

But, the car left at last and, seconds later, he darted out of the drive and down the road.

Gran. He needed his gran. He'd always been able to talk to her . . .

His grandparents were working in the garden when he got there. His grandfather looked up with a slow, warm smile of pleasure and surprise.

"Hello, young Jim! I didn't know you were coming today." He glanced down the road. "Where's your mum?"

"She's gone out with Matt and Lucy," James said, his throat tightening uncomfortably. "I said I didn't want to go. I wanted to see you." It was nearly true, he told himself.

HIS grandad's smile broadened.

"Did you now! Well, that's handy for both of us. I could do with some help."

"Now, Bill, you're not using James as slave labour," Audrey chided.

"It's OK, Gran, I don't mind," James said. "Well, not for a bit, anyway."

James turned to his grandfather, who soon had him weeding and raking and carrying rubbish to the bin.

"Your dad used to help in the garden when he was your age," Bill said.

Gran and Grandad never minded talking about his father. Sometimes they talked as if he were still here, still part of them, which was

AFTER the failure of the 1715 Jacobite Rising there had been great despondency among the Royal exiles in Holland, and the arrival of a baby son to the deposed King and his Queen was a cause not only for rejoicing but also for new hope that the British throne could yet be regained.

So it was that the destiny of the young Prince Charles Edward Stuart was already mapped out. He was a fine-looking boy, knew what was expected of him, and as he grew to manhood he was all enthusiasm to make a second bid to reinstate his father as King.

The actual campaign of the 1745 Rising started on the shores of France, from where the Prince's ships set out, intending to make a landing on the coast of Scotland. Unfortunately, the ship carrying a heavy load of arms was attacked by a more powerful Government vessel, and had to return to France in a crippled state.

The Prince's own ship heaved to in the Hebrides, just off the little island of Eriskay, and it was there that he first set foot on Scottish soil. Alas, his friends and advisers, seven honest men and true, told him that, without arms and equipment, the Rising was doomed from the start, and that he should return home forthwith.

"But I am come home," the Prince said. He had no thought of retreat. The first step was made.

Visit the lovely little island of Eriskay, and you can tread the "Prince's strand" (Coilleag á Phrionnsa) where Bonnie Prince Charlie came ashore on July 23, 1745.

Look around near the beach and you may find a little convolvulus flower, a rarity of the Hebrides. Local folk call it the "Prince's Flower."

And no doubt you will remember the Eriskay Love-Lilt, loveliest of all Hebridean songs.

nice, James thought, because in a way he *was* still part of them.

He wondered if Mum marrying Matt would change that. But he was too busy in the garden to worry about it. In fact, he was having such a good time that it came as a shock when his grandad said it was time to stop.

"I don't overwork my helpers, whatever your grandmother might think," he said cheerfully. "Now then — payment. Will the usual rates be OK?"

James nodded.

"Right, then, off you go and ask your gran for one of those bars of chocolate out of the fridge."

"Thanks, Grandad." He hurried into the house.

"Hello, Gran. I've finished helping in the garden and Grandad says I can have some chocolate."

"I should think so, too." Audrey rose with a loving smile, fetched a bar of chocolate and a glass of orange juice, and sat down

21

again. "There, that should keep you going."

"Thanks, Gran." James unwrapped the chocolate and broke the first few pieces. He offered one to Gran, who smiled and shook her head. He knew he should keep a piece for Grandad when he came in — it *was* his chocolate, after all.

James liked sharing. He always shared his sweets with Mum, and with Lucy, who sometimes wanted more than James felt like giving her, and back in the old days, he'd shared them with Dad. Soon, he supposed he'd be sharing them with Matt . . .

Then he remembered why he'd come here today, and the whole world seemed to stop.

"James?" his gran said from miles away. "What's wrong, love?"

"Nothing," James whispered. "I was just . . . just thinking . . ." Then, painfully, the words came. "You know Mum's going to marry Matthew . . ."

"Yes, I know," Gran said.

"Do you think it's all right?" James looked up, eyes huge. "I mean, do you think Dad would mind?"

Audrey said nothing for a moment. Rising, she carried James' glass across to the sink. Then she turned.

"No, I don't think he'd mind," she said simply. "I don't think he'd mind at all.

"Do *you* mind?" she asked very gently. "I thought you liked Matthew . . ."

"I do," James said wretchedly. "It's nothing to do with not liking him — it's just . . . Dad told me to look after them. That day before he went away, he told me to look after Mum and Lucy. And I wondered if — whether . . ."

"If you needed to make sure this was right?" Audrey said softly. "If your dad would have thought it was right?"

James nodded numbly, fighting tears. Audrey took his hand.

"It's not been easy for any of us, love," she said gently. "We all still miss your dad terribly.

"I was very sad when he died," she went on. "He was my son, you see, and I knew and cared for him right from when he was born, from when he was a child just like you.

"You see, you don't expect your children to die before you. They're supposed to grow up and grow old and live on after you. So if they don't it's very sad, because it feels all wrong . . .

"But there are other things that don't make me sad," she added.

"What, Gran?"

"You." Gran smiled lovingly. "You and your mum and Lucy — the most precious things your dad ever gave me.

"You're all part of him, you see, because you're his family. You're part of his life and his world. And while I've got you I can never lose him."

"But it won't be the same with Matt," James whispered.

"No, love, it won't," Audrey said, squeezing his hand. "But that's life — that's what happens. Right through your life, you'll find that things change, but as long as you've got people to love you, you'll be OK.

"And lots of people love you. Me and your grandad, your mum, even little Lucy . . . and now there's Matt, as well."

"You mean Dad wouldn't mind?"

"I'm sure he wouldn't," Audrey said gently. "He'd be glad that your mum's going to be happy again. And he'd be gladder still that you'll have someone to help you look after them."

To help him look after them . . .

OUT in the hall, the phone rang.
"I shan't be a minute," Audrey said cheerfully. "You finish your chocolate — and don't worry."

She left the kitchen to answer the phone. Through the half-open door, James heard every word she said.

"Caroline!" It was his mother. "Yes, he's been here all afternoon. I think he needed to talk . . ." And then her voice dropped, and James couldn't hear any more.

"OK, love. Don't worry. We'll be waiting. Goodbye." There was a click, then Audrey returned to the kitchen.

James suddenly felt very small.

"You didn't tell your mum you were coming here, did you?"

He shook his head, eyes huge. Then suddenly the words poured out.

"I couldn't, Gran. I know it was wrong and I'm sorry, but I couldn't tell her. I wanted to see you, I wanted to talk —"

"I know, love. I know." Audrey smiled. "And your mum understands, too. Don't worry. It's all going to work out, love — you'll see."

They waited and his mother soon arrived. She hurried into the kitchen with little Lucy sound asleep in her arms.

"Oh, James, I was worried about you," his mum said. She didn't look cross, she just looked relieved. "I didn't know what to think when we turned up at Robin's and they said they hadn't seen you. I wondered where you were."

"I'm sorry, Mum. I didn't mean to . . ."

"It's OK, love, I know. Just as long as you're all right . . ."

"He is," his gran said softly. "He's going to be fine."

James looked at her, then looked at his family. They were so loved, so familiar. Yet something was missing — he wasn't sure what. Then Matthew came in, and suddenly he knew.

They were his family, all of them. They were Dad's family, and now they were Matthew's, too . . .

"I'm sorry, Matthew," he whispered. Then he felt Matthew's arms around him, loving and forgiving and gentle and safe. His heart swelled. It would be all right, he thought — everything would be all right.

The wedding wouldn't change anything, because there was nothing to change. Without even thinking, he was going home with them. . . □

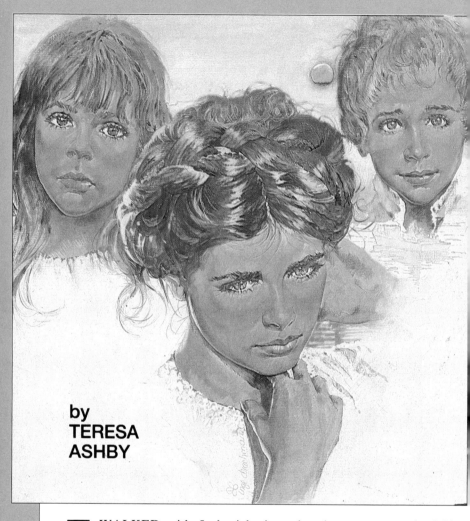

by
TERESA
ASHBY

I WALKED with Josh right into the classroom, proud of him from the toes of his shiny black shoes to the ends of his gleaming blond hair.

He held tight to my hand for a moment, then recognised one or two faces from playgroup, and he was off without so much as a backward glance.

With tears blinding me, I made my escape.

As I was leaving, I saw a little girl on her way in. The dress she wore was too tight, the shabby cardigan too big. She looked little and scared and I wanted to scoop her up in my arms and give her a hug!

I held the door open for her and she stepped inside.

"Is your mum coming?" I asked, because I couldn't think that

Like Father, Like Son

anyone would send a child so young to school on their own —
especially on their first day.

"Mum's still in bed," she said, with a shake of her head.

Then the eagle-eyed teacher saw her and came across. Enfolding
her in her arms, she drew her into the bright warmth of the
classroom, welcoming her.

Thank goodness for teachers like that, I thought as I hurried away.
And that's when it all came flooding back to me . . .

It was such a beautiful day and I knew the house would feel empty
without Josh. I stopped in the park and sat down. The air was
fragrant with the scent of hundreds of spring flowers and despite the
chill breeze, I could feel the warmth from the sun.

Like Josh, I had my first day at school following the Easter
holiday. Unlike him, I didn't know a soul and was gripped by a
nameless terror.

Mum had to leave me in the playground with all the other children.
That was the way things were then. There was none of this going
right into the classroom with your child.

I stood alone in the playground, tears running down my face. To
this day, I can remember how alone and frightened I felt. It still
makes me shiver.

It was cold that Easter — and damp, too. It had been raining and
the playground was covered in puddles.

An older boy charged past, stamped in a puddle and filled my nice
new shoes with icy, dirty water. Some had splattered my skirt, my
lovely new skirt, and my white socks were streaked with grey.

"Cry-baby!" he taunted as I began to blubber.

Other children came to look, as children will, and soon I was surrounded. I howled my eyes out, feeling as if my world had come to an end.

The girls were worst. Some of them pushed me, making me cry even more.

SUDDENLY there was an arm around my shoulders. I looked up at a face streaked with dirt and hair that looked as if it had never seen a comb — and the brightest, bluest eyes I'd ever seen.

His arm tightened around me as he hit out with his free hand at the other kids.

"Leave her alone!" he yelled. And added a few other things which, when I repeated them to my mother, made her throw her hands up in horror.

The crowd began to break up as a huge, fearsome-looking woman appeared. She had a large, angry face and a mouth so twisted, it brought all my terror rushing back.

"You again, Soames!" she bellowed at my rescuer.

I thought he'd shrink away, but he stood up to her.

"Look what they done to 'er!" He pushed me forward. "She looked so pretty, an' all."

She turned to me.

"You're the new girl aren't you? Beverly Graham? Well, stop snivelling and get inside. The bell went ages ago and you're late!"

The fearsome woman turned out to be my class teacher and, because of what had happened in the playground, she took an instant dislike to me. The morning was awful.

Then my first school dinner. Another nightmare, with soggy greens, chewy meat and lumpy potatoes.

The other children poked fun at me when I tried to refuse to eat it. Again, Mark Soames came to my rescue.

He showed me a hole in the playground wall after dinner and I scrambled through it after him. We sat on the railway embankment watching the freight trains rumbling by. My clothes got muddy — but I didn't care any more.

The Telephone Call

What a jumble of sound,
Not a word could I hear,
As I held the receiver,
Close to my ear.
A faulty line? Oh no, not true,
My darling grandson, not yet two.

— M. L. Temple.

"We're from two different ends of a rainbow, we are," Mark told me.

"I live over there . . ." He waved his hand in the direction of some grimy, soot-blackened cottages on the other side of the track. "An' you come from a posh house."

My house certainly wasn't posh. It was just a modest semi, with a pretty garden. But I suppose, to someone like Mark, it must have seemed so.

"I bet your dad spoils you," he went on. "Me dad ran off, so I look after Mum now. She thinks he's coming home, but he's gone for good and I'm glad. She's not well, that's why me clothes ain't very clean."

He plucked at the sleeve of his ragged jumper.

"I do the shopping and that — but I don't know how to do washing."

"Don't you just put it in the machine?" I suggested.

He roared with laughter and ruffled my hair with a grubby hand.

"You're a riot, you are! Washing machine — are you kidding?"

"What did you mean about the rainbow?" I blushed.

"Your end's got the pot of gold and my end is in the . . ." He broke off and grinned. "My end is in the muck."

WHEN Mum came for me at the end of the day, I couldn't stop talking about my new friend. She seemed pleased as I skipped along beside her, telling her how he'd rescued me.

I didn't tell her we'd spent the lunch break sitting on the railway embankment. Somehow, I didn't think she'd approve.

"Perhaps you could invite him home for tea one day," she said. "What's his name?"

When I told her, she stopped in her tracks.

"But he's — he's —" She stared at me, shocked. "He's not a nice boy."

"He is!" I leapt to his defence as he had leapt to mine. "He's funny and he looks after me!"

"You're to stay away from him," she said with a loud sniff. "He's always getting into trouble and his mother's a —"

It was her own fault for abandoning me in the playground in the first place! She wasn't there to look after me — but Mark was.

"They're not very clean people, Beverly," she told me when we'd started walking. "I'd really rather you didn't mix with him."

"So he can't come for tea then?" I asked cheekily.

"Certainly not!" She shuddered. "Why don't you ask someone nice? One of the girls?"

One of the girls that laughed at me for crying? No thank you!

Because I'd been forbidden to play with him — because he always stuck up for me . . . and because I liked him, Mark remained my best friend! It was the first time I'd ever *really* defied my mother.

I paid close attention when she gossiped about Mrs Soames.

I heard how Mark sat on the cold stone steps outside the pub, waiting for her. And how he'd been caught pinching sweets.

"He's a cunning little monkey," my mother's friend, Brenda said. "He knows the police can't touch him until he's older! But they will! You mark my words, that boy will end up in prison."

I was horrified. They couldn't send Mark to prison, could they? Tearfully, I begged him not to steal things any more.

"It was only a bar of chocolate," he said. "I couldn't help meself. It just sort of happened. But don't cry, I won't do it again. I promise."

And, as far as I knew, he kept that promise.

Gradually, I made friends among the girls in my own age group and I saw less and less of Mark. He was growing up, growing away and he eventually left to go to the big school.

I saw him once, waiting for the bus. His trousers were too short and flapped above his ankles. His shoes were scuffed, the laces frayed and the anorak he wore was snagged and full of holes.

He stood apart from the others at the bus stop, his hands thrust deep in his pockets. He looked proud — but miserable.

I looked at the other boys. They had neatly pressed trousers and smart blazers and I walked the rest of the way to my school with tears streaming down my face.

Mark didn't have a dirty face any more and his long hair was always combed — but he couldn't do anything about his shabby clothes.

By the time I went to the big school, I had lots of friends and was happily confident. I was growing up, turning into a young lady.

Clothes became vitally important and I started to experiment with make-up.

I even got a crush on one of the boys in the year above mine! It was all very exciting and wonderful until . . .

We were sitting on the grass, about eight of us, eating our packed lunches and chatting and giggling.

Then I noticed a lonely figure standing a little way away. He looked at me, then started to come over. I shrank. It was Mark.

"Hello, Bev." He grinned — his old, friendly grin. "Settling in all right?"

My friends gaped in horror. Some of them giggled. Suddenly it seemed that everyone had fallen silent and was watching . . . waiting . . . I had to save face somehow.

"What's it to you?" I said as snootily as I could.

"You remember me, don't you?" His grin started to waver slightly. "Mark . . . Mark Soames."

I thought of all the times we'd sat on the railway embankment sharing our wishes and dreams. I recalled how he'd said, with quiet vehemence, that when he grew up and had kids, they'd have new clothes, not second-hand — and shoes that fitted and socks that didn't fall down.

I remembered how he'd been my only friend for such a long time . . . But these were my friends now.

"Oh, I remember," I said. "Haven't you got a washing machine yet?"

I waved my hand in front of my face and rolled my eyes. The other girls fell about, but when I looked at Mark, he looked . . . crushed. I've never seen anyone look so hurt.

I didn't laugh. I would have done anything to take the words back. Even now, when I think about it, I feel ashamed and angry.

It taught me something, though. Saying things like that, hurtful things, don't just wound the person they're intended for. Words like that leave scars behind.

After that, if I was ever tempted to say something hasty, I bit my tongue.

I FELT a spot of rain hit my face, then another, and got up quickly from the park bench. I'd have to run home if I wasn't going to get a soaking.

The house did seem empty without Josh.

He has two older sisters, but this was the first time I'd been so alone. When Tasha started school, I had Lori to look after, then when Lori started, there was Josh. Now there was just me and the dog!

I cleaned the place from top to bottom and, when I stopped for lunch, I wondered how Josh was managing at school.

He'd been delighted with his Thunderbirds lunch box and had helped me pack it that morning. I hoped he'd manage to open his flask . . .

After lunch, I sat down with a book to pass the time until I could go and fetch Josh. The words on the page kept blurring.

I was thinking of Mark again. He'd left school and joined the Army. It wasn't long after that that his mother died.

He wore his uniform for her funeral. He was the only mourner. Mrs Soames had no friends, no family . . .

For the first time in my life, I wondered about her. What tragedy had made her the way she was? And what was it about human nature that made people mock and jeer at her when they should have been helping her?

I watched from the cemetery gate and would have hurried away, but Mark saw me and came over. He looked tall and handsome in his uniform.

"I'm sorry," I said. "About your mum . . ."

"She didn't have much of a life. Maybe she's better off where she is. It can't be any worse than it was here, can it?"

I shook my head. After what I'd said to him that day at school, it was a wonder he didn't hate me. Yet, here he was, looking as if he was really pleased to see me!

"Is it nice? In the Army, I mean?" I asked.

"Yes. For the first time in my life, I feel as good as everyone else. I'm training as an engineer so, when I come out, I'll be able to get a decent job. Might even get myself a house on your street!"

The vicar passed us and said goodbye. For a few minutes, we were alone.

"Come on, love." Mark took my hand. "Let's get away from here."

IT was time to fetch Josh. I hurried to the school and waited impatiently outside the classroom with several other anxious parents.

The children were sitting on a big rug listening as the teacher told a story. I looked through the window in the door and could see Josh, sitting cross-legged next to the little girl in the tight dress.

He was such a warm-hearted little soul. I knew that, if she was feeling unsure of herself, he'd take care of her.

At last, they got up and went to fetch their coats. They flooded out of the doors in a noisy, gabbling flood.

Josh came out clutching the little girl's hand.

"Can Sophie come to tea?" he asked.

"Of course, she can. But we'd better check with her mum first."

Sophie's little face lit up. It wasn't a very clean little face, but she had a determined look about her that I'd seen before. In Mark. He'd always been determined not to stay at the grotty end of the rainbow.

"I can't wait to see Dad," Josh said excitedly. "I want to sing him this song I learned today!"

"You only have to wait until tea-time." I laughed. "You can always sing it to Tasha and Lori when we get home!"

Mark was closing the garage early today. Nothing would stop him hearing all about his son's first day at school! He was a father first and foremost and, just as he'd always vowed, his children always had clean, shiny shoes and decent clothes.

"Our house is called Rainbow's End. What's yours called?" Josh asked his new little friend.

"It ain't got a name," Sophie replied. "It's got a number. Number three."

"We've got a number, too," Josh said earnestly. "Ours is number eight."

As we were walking away, the classroom door opened and the teacher came out.

"Is something wrong?" I asked.

"Oh, no, not at all." She smiled. "Josh left his lunch-box behind."

She handed it to me and smiled sadly at Sophie, who had walked a little way ahead with Josh.

"You should be very proud of him, Mrs Soames."

"I am. He's got a warm heart — like his dad." Like my dearest Mark.

As I walked home with my boy, my heart felt so swollen with love and pride, I thought it might burst!

We'd found our pot of gold. It was there in our children, in our home and in our love for each other.

Our very own Rainbow's End. □

by AUDREY E. GROOM

HARRY was sixty-six, retired, fit as a fiddle and had been a widower for the last four years.

He wasn't a lonely man, far from it. He belonged to the bowls club and a gardening club. He had good neighbours and a number of friends.

His daughter lived abroad and his son at the other end of the country, but they phoned often, and Rob brought his family to visit two or three times a year. So life should have been tolerable.

But to Harry, it wasn't.

Since Marjorie had died, it had seemed to have no meaning whatsoever.

Preparing meals for one; decorating rooms no-one else cared about; watching television, without anyone to discuss it with; walking, yet not being able to share the green and gold of spring and the browns of autumn — living alone brought little enjoyment.

One or two of his associates at the bowling club, in the same position, had married for the second time, and encouraged him to do the same.

"One happy marriage is the foundation for another," his old

One Afternoon In Spring

friend, Bert, told him. "There're lots of attractive ladies about, Harry. You could be happy again with one of them, I'm sure."

Bert was partly right.

There were lots of personable mature ladies, almost everywhere Harry went. But though Harry enjoyed a chat or a game of bowls, or dancing with them at social evenings, there wasn't one of them that he would dream of putting in Marjorie's place.

"You were unique, love," he told her photograph, as he stood holding it one wonderful spring afternoon. He was looking out at his own colourful garden, glorious with forsythia, daffodils and pink blossom. As all the villages round about would be now.

He thought, nostalgically, of times in the past when the weather had been like this. He and Marjorie, both keen photographers, would take their cameras and, armed with sandwiches and tea, go out to explore the countryside and try to capture its beauty.

Wonderful days they were!

He looked over at the bookshelf where his camera lay, unused since the last time Rob had brought the grandchildren.

In fact, the shots that were in there were probably out of date now. He picked the camera up.

Yes, there was half a roll of film still to use. Well, why not use it? At least he'd get the shots printed before those toddlers started work!

He smiled at his own thoughts as he went out to the car.

It really was a superb day. Isn't it surprising, Harry reflected, that spring comes every year and yet we're still amazed at its shine, its colour and its glory. Almost as though we were seeing it for the first time.

HE stopped in one village after another, photographing flowers, thatched cottages, two cats sitting together on a wall and a dog lying stretched out in the sun.

Nothing mindblowing there, he thought ruefully. He and Marjorie would have searched for more unusual angles. But he'd lost the incentive to do that. These would be pretty pictures, that was all.

He saw a garden centre signposted, and decided to go and look around. Not with a great deal of enthusiasm, but something might take his fancy.

He made his way through to the rose section, and crouched down to look at the labels.

Suddenly he was aware of someone else doing the same thing. A woman, probably a little younger than himself, small, neat, wearing jeans and a sweater.

"Unusual names, haven't they?" she said and read out, "Lively Cara, Pride of the Castle, Melanie's Choice."

Her voice was deep for her small stature, and musical. Harry found himself smiling as they both stood up, and he discovered that she hardly reached to his shoulder.

She was quite ordinary to look at, with brown, slightly greying hair.

One Afternoon In Spring

"They certainly are," Harry agreed. "Must have been grown by a poet, I should think."

Her smile transformed her face, lighting her eyes. Her mouth was wide and generous.

"I only know about Peace and Ena Harkness." She laughed, and moved away down the path.

He had a ridiculous urge to follow her. His mind, rusty in this sort of situation, refused to come up with anything else to say.

He watched her disappear into the flowering shrubs and perennials section, feeling bereft, for no good reason, and bent again to examine the roses.

He chose two and carried them towards the check-out, looking around as he did so, vaguely aware of a feeling of disappointment.

Near the check-out were some beautiful cyclamen plants in delicate and unusual colours.

He put the roses on the pay-desk and went back for a cyclamen. He hadn't a clue why, because he wasn't into houseplants at all.

With his purchases stowed in the car, he thought, where now? Home? Or on to the next village?

He had a vague memory that there was a pleasant tea-room there. He felt he needed a cup of tea.

Ethel's Pantry was still there.

"There's a garden at the back, dear," said the comfortable woman. "Go on through, and I'll come out and take your order."

AFTER the darkness of the shop, the garden was dazzling. As he stood for a moment, shading his eyes from the sunlight and wondering where to sit, he suddenly smiled.

There she was! The woman from the garden centre. And alone.

He felt a ridiculous happiness flood through him as he approached her table. She was reading, and only looked up as his shadow darkened her page.

"Hello!" he said.

"Oh! Hello!"

Did she recognise him, or was she just being polite?

"May I?" He indicated the free chair.

"Yes, of course."

Her eyes flicked back to her book, and for a moment they sat in silence. He wanted to know what she was reading. He wanted to know very much.

Then, as the café owner advanced on them she closed the book, and he saw it was a Hardy novel. He loved Hardy.

"Er — could we share a pot of tea?" he suggested.

The woman nodded.

"And a cream cake?" she said, with a smile.

"For me, too."

It was now or never, before she went back to her book.

"Beautiful day, isn't it?" he began.

"Spring's more wonderful every year," she agreed.

"I was only thinking that at lunch-time."

33

C

"Were you? Great minds, you know," she said, and smiled again. "Did you buy a rose-bush?"

"No. Did you?"

"Yes, two and —" He hesitated, remembering the pot-plant, and knew he wanted to give it to her. But he couldn't, could he? Well, not until after tea anyway.

"After tea" was nearly an hour away.

It turned out to be a delightful tea. Harry and Helen discussed roses and books, springtime and music, food, and (surprise, surprise) photography.

"Yes, I have a camera. Don't use it often. Need a bit of tuition, I'm afraid."

They had both parked in the local carpark, and walked across to it together.

Could he offer her the plant? Harry hesitated.

He did.

"Well, thank you so much, it's beautiful, but I —" She blushed furiously, but she seemed pleased.

He took a deep breath.

"And would you perhaps — that is — would you come out with me one evening? A meal — the pictures — whatever you like?"

When she didn't answer immediately, he put out a hand and touched hers.

"Please," he said, "please say yes."

Hours later, back home, happy with Helen's answer, and even happier with the way he felt, Harry found himself tracing her name on a piece of paper, much as he had done as a lad when a girl had taken his fancy.

Only Helen was no chit of a girl, but a mature woman, as he was a mature man.

He suspected that this wasn't just a taking of his fancy, but more like — dare he say it? Dare he think it? It was like falling in love.

There was the special, essential element that just hadn't been there with any of those other nice, kind, attractive matrons he had met before.

Well, he mustn't leap his fences. He and Helen would have to meet often, and get to know each other better — their likes, dislikes, moods, high and lows. You couldn't rush things, even if you were pretty hopeful of the outcome.

But neither must they wait too long. As the old song said, "It's a long, long time from May till September, and the days grow short . . ." but not too short.

Harry had a feeling he and Helen would enjoy many happy days together.

"You're still unique, sweetheart," he said to Marjorie's photo, "because you understand, don't you!"

He slept that night like a man half his age and awoke to a feeling that was strange to him.

He was happy . . . ☐

ON WINGS OF LOVE

by DAVID BRYANT

PEGGY COLES settled herself uneasily into seat number G 17. She hadn't flown before, and she wasn't looking forward to the experience.

"It's the safest form of travel, Mum," her daughter, Anis, had tried to reassure her. "You're much more likely to have an accident driving down the M1, you know."

But that hadn't taken away the nervousness. What if the engines seize up? Or perhaps the plane would be struck by lightning? Or the pilot will have a heart attack . . . ?

Nothing would have induced Peggy to take that flight to Gibraltar, if Anis hadn't just given birth to a son, Adam. He was the first grandchild in the family and she just had to see him!

If only she could have got there without flying! But it would take far too long, and she didn't want to leave Frank on his own longer than was absolutely necessary.

All around her, passengers were stacking luggage in the overhead compartments and fastening safety belts. She watched a businessman in a pinstripe suit settle confidently down and pick up a pile of correspondence. She envied him his calm.

She turned her head and looked out of the window, relishing her last moments on solid ground.

The seat next to her was only filled at the very last moment. A young woman, who didn't look more than a schoolgirl to Peggy, made her way down the aisle.

"G 18," she said. "Is it this one?"

"Well, I'm G 17, so I think that must be right," Peggy smiled.

The girl was holding a small baby, a new plastic hold-all and several carrier bags. Her face was chalky white, and she looked decidedly unhappy.

"This is the plane for Gibraltar, isn't it?"

"That's right, my dear."

"My husband is over there." The girl seemed over-anxious to talk. "He's in the Army. We've just been given our first married quarters."

She looked at Peggy, weighing her up, and seeing a kind, smiling face, she went on.

"I . . . I haven't flown before. Will you make sure I'm OK? I'm a bit scared, to be honest."

Join the club, Peggy thought. But the girl really did look terrified, and her motherly instincts were aroused. This lass was even worse than she was.

She had a quick look round to see if any of the cabin staff were free, but they were all busy getting the passengers settled, ready for take-off.

Swallowing the fear that kept rising in her throat, she spoke with a confidence that she didn't feel.

"Of course I will, dear. There's nothing to worry about." She remembered her daughter's words. "Flying is the safest form of transport. You're more likely to have an accident driving along the motorway."

"Is that right?" The girl's need for reassurance was touching.

Peggy decided to embark on an enormous white lie.

"I know the drill. I'll make sure you're all right." She took a deep breath and told an even bigger one.

"Once you've done it a few times, you don't think anything of it."

"You've flown a lot of times, then?" The girl perked up at once.

Peggy fielded this one skilfully.

"Well, I'm much older than you, dear." She beamed.

THE aircraft began to taxi, and the hostess turned on some cheerful music. Peggy sneaked a quick look round the cabin. The passengers were calmly chewing sweets, doing crosswords or reading books.

They reached the holding bay, paused for a second or two, and then the pilot revved the engines to full power. There was a punching feeling in the small of Peggy's back, and the aircraft began to race along the runway.

The girl looked terrified. Her face was greenish white, and her hands were shaking.

Peggy had no time to think of herself. Her attention was needed elsewhere.

She took the girl's hand and began to talk, quietly and reassuringly.

"Now what's your name, love? Tracy? I've got a niece called Tracy. She'll be seven next week. A pretty, fair-haired little thing and

Part 2

NEXT day, leaving Eriskay, the Prince and his friends landed on the Scottish mainland at Loch Of The Caves near Arisaig. They received a warm welcome, and all were taken with Charles Edward's princely air and enthusiasm for the Royal cause.

The Prince then went north to the Highlands to meet the various clan Chieftains, and prepare the way for the raising of an army. Some of the clansmen were doubtful about taking part in so precarious a campaign, but the Prince's inspiring manner soon won them over.

A gathering of the clans was fixed, and the Prince's trail now leads to Glenfinnan at the head of Loch Shiel for the Raising of the Standard. All went well. Resentment against the English forces for their treatment of the clans in the aftermath of the 1715 Rising fired the Highlanders into action, and Sir John Cope, who had a Government army in Scotland at the same time, decided to withdraw southwards and watch events.

But it wasn't long before the Highland army caught up with him, and this they did at Prestonpans.

up to all kinds of tricks.

"And your baby's name? Stuart? He's a bonnie boy, all right. He's got your eyes, too. Bright blue. And what a head of hair! They always say, 'Born with a thatch of hair and never a care'."

The plane reached the end of the runway and began to climb steeply. The baby broke into a high-pitched screaming, hating the pressure on his ear drums.

Peggy knew all about this. The week before, she had borrowed a book from the library on flying and there had been a whole paragraph on how to deal with crying babies during landing and take-off.

She decided to keep Tracy busy, take her mind off things.

"It's the pressure that's making him cry, Tracy. Have you got a bottle? If he has a good suck it will stop his ears hurting."

She neatly lifted the baby off Tracy's lap once the plane levelled out, freeing the girl to search in one of the carrier bags. Tracy unearthed spare nappies, tinned milk, baby clothes, and there was the bottle, right at the bottom of the heap.

She handed it to Peggy, and baby Stuart sucked eagerly. The crying gave way to whimpering, and then a contented purring sound.

"There," Peggy said. "He's fine now."

Tracy was still white, but the activity had done her good. A fleeting smile touched her face.

"Thanks. I wouldn't have known what was wrong. He's a terrible crier, is Stuart, specially when he's out of his routine."

All at once she seemed less nervous. She began to talk nineteen to the dozen.

Peggy learnt all about Corporal John Mackintosh, who was stationed in Gibraltar, and who was thrilled to bits at the thought of seeing his first child.

She had a rundown on Corporal Mackintosh's last five letters, and was even asked to read the one written after the phone call telling him of Stuart's birth.

Best of all, Tracy asked her if she would like to nurse the baby, and she had a delectable half-hour holding the tiny bundle in her arms.

She was pleased to find that she hadn't forgotten the art of being a mother. She'd need the skill herself, when she reached Gibraltar and saw her own grandchild for the first time.

All of this took her mind off the jigsaw of fields and roads and miniature towns, which she could see far below. What with one thing and another, she hardly had time to think about failing engines and pilots with cardiac arrests.

THE turbulence started over the Bay of Biscay and Peggy, scared out of her wits, took a look at young Tracy.

Her face had turned the old familiar green, and she was shaking like a leaf.

"Are we going to crash?" she whispered, clutching at Peggy's arm.

Peggy took a deep breath. "Of course not. It's just a few air pockets. The Bay of Biscay's notorious for them."

She wasn't at all sure about this, but it sounded good, and she had to say something to calm the girl down.

The baby chose to dirty his nappy just as the aeroplane dropped like an express lift. It was the only time in Peggy's life that she could remember being actually pleased at the thought of handling a soiled nappy!

"There's not much room, Tracy, and we can't take his seat-belt off, so we'll have to work together. You get out a fresh nappy and I'll slip this one off.

"Now see if you can find a rusk. We don't want Stuart to start crying. Have you got a plastic bag for the old nappy? And where's the baby powder?"

She kept up a steady stream of chatter halfway across the Bay of Biscay. By the time they had finished, the weather had calmed down, and Stuart was dressed again, sucking his thumb contentedly.

Peggy was beginning to feel exhausted from keeping Tracy's spirits up, but she couldn't collapse yet! There was another hour to go before landing — the pilot had just announced it over the public address system.

The plane began its descent towards Gibraltar. The engine note died down, and there was a roar as the landing gear was lowered.

Peggy said an inward prayer, but Tracy leaned over towards her and buried her face in her jacket.

"I'm scared," said a tiny voice.

PEGGY put aside her worries and made a heroic effort to talk Tracy through it all.

"We'll be down in a few minutes, Tracy, and won't your John be glad to see you? Just imagine his face when he sees Stuart.

"And what about that new house? You'll have fun getting things just the way you want them . . ." She held Tracy close, willing the girl to draw comfort from her.

They descended lower and lower, skimming the top of a mountain, flirting across a road, and then came a bump and roar of sound as the pilot applied reverse thrust.

Peggy let out her breath in a slow, sigh of sheer relief. Down at last. Safely on the ground.

She lifted the girl's head and brushed the loose strands of hair back from the white face.

"We're down safely, Tracy. A good flight, and right on time.

"Now you find a mirror and touch up that lipstick, ready for John. Where's Stuart's bootee? It must have slipped under the seat."

Already the colour was returning to Tracy's cheeks. She looked a different person, smiling and excited.

"Thank you so much for looking after me, Peggy. I couldn't have managed without you, honest. I'd have been scared to death if you hadn't been sitting next to me!"

"I've enjoyed talking to you," Peggy said. "It's brightened up the flight no end."

It had, too. If she hadn't been able to look after the baby and care for Tracy, Peggy would have been a nervous wreck herself.

They walked together through the arrival lounge, past customs and passport control, and out into the main hall.

Peggy waited just long enough to see Tracy throw herself into the arms of a smart, young man in uniform, and then hustled forward through the crowd, searching for her daughter.

Anis was waiting there, under the clock, holding baby Adam in her arms. Peggy hugged and kissed them both. She had tears in her eyes as she proudly took her grandson in her arms for the first time.

"It's lovely to see you, Mum. What sort of flight did you have? I hope you weren't frightened?"

"Frightened, Anis? There wasn't time for that. I've been far too busy! I'll tell you about it later."

Anis led the way out of the terminal building into the hot, heady Mediterranean sunshine.

"Welcome to Gibraltar, Mum. I'm sure you'll love it."

Peggy was sure, too. Ahead of her lay two wonderful weeks with Anis, Alan and Adam, in their new house. It was going to be the holiday of a lifetime — and quite possibly the first of many! □

AS she took the next box from the van, Linda became aware that she was being watched. She turned quickly, to see a tall, lean figure on the far side of the lane.

He smiled as their eyes met but before Linda could speak he raised his battered cap in greeting and strode off up the gentle hill.

She took the box into the back shop, wondering vaguely who the man was. She'd met very few of the villagers so far.

"Hello. Is there anyone at home?"

The gentle voice startled Linda. She set down the box of china with a thump that shook the table.

"Yes, can I help you?" She stepped out into the shop proper to greet the uninvited guests.

There were two of them: a small, willowy woman in her sixties and a distinguished-looking man who leaned heavily on a stick. She didn't recognise either, but then she'd only been in the village three days.

Linda had spent long hours agonising over whether she was doing the right thing. After the break-up of her marriage, going back to her pottery, to the only thing she felt really good at, seemed the right thing to do.

Now that she had made the move, and started to discover all the unforeseen problems of opening a shop, she no longer felt quite so sure.

But the time had been right to get away from the city, from the countless familiar places and faces, constant reminders of the lie her old life had turned out to be.

And then, of course, there was Emma. Living in the country would be so much better for her little daughter.

"My name's Hilda Peeks and this is Wing Commander Clitheroe. We represent the parish council." The woman smiled. "We thought we would take this opportunity to welcome you to the village, Miss . . ."

"Wood," Linda said quickly. "Linda Wood."

"It's good to see the old bakery in use again." The Wing Commander offered a dry, long-fingered hand.

"I run the post office and village store, across the lane there, so we'll be neighbours." The old lady ran a calculating eye around the craft shop as she spoke. "Although not competitors, I see."

"We wish you every success," the Wing Commander said sincerely.

WELCOME

"Thank you." Linda was interrupted as the shop door burst open.

"Mum, there's a great big ginger cat sitting on our wall! He's lovely, come and see." Emma stopped suddenly, as she became aware of the visitors.

"This is my daughter Emma," Linda supplied. "She starts at the village school next Monday, don't you?"

The Wing Commander stooped to her level.

"That sounds like the General," he said quietly. "The General is the biggest, fattest cat in the whole village."

"He is very big," Emma whispered.

"The General is the chief of all the animals hereabouts. He's welcoming you to the village, and that's a great honour." The old man held out a hand. "Let's just make sure."

Linda smiled approval, and the little girl led him quickly outside.

by
PAUL
KNIGHT

HOME

Linda felt a wave of gratitude. It was such a simple thing, but she knew it would mean more to Emma than a thousand welcomes.

Emma was still deeply hurt and confused from the sudden loss of her dad. She'd thought, to start with, it was her fault. Kindness like the Wing Commander's would help the process of healing.

Suddenly all Linda's doubts began to fade. Perhaps moving had been the right thing to do after all.

"He's soft as a brush, you know."

"Sorry?" Linda looked up, but Hilda was gazing wistfully out through the window.

"The Wing Commander — Charles. The original crusty old bachelor. Children are his weak spot."

Linda allowed herself a small smile. Crusty old bachelors seemed to be someone else's weak spot!

By the end of the first week, most of the stock was in place, and the workroom, complete with kiln, was up and running. The flat upstairs felt like home. All that was needed to complete the transformation was a new sign.

G OOD morning, Miss Peeks."
The old woman smiled as Linda and Emma walked into the post office. "The name's Hilda, my dear. What can I do for you today?"

"Well, I'm looking for a bit of help, actually. I'm looking for a sign writer to redo the shop sign. The ones in the phone box are booked up for weeks. I just wondered if you might know someone local?"

"There's Steady's grandson, I suppose. Although I'm not sure if he does signs."

"Steady?"

Hilda laughed at Linda's confusion. "Oh, we have a nickname for everyone around here. Steady is Edward Ormerod. He's a gardener. He was a hero during the war . . . His grandson's a boat painter. They live down on the wides."

Again she smiled at Linda's look of consternation.

"The canal, my dear, the far side of the village. They live in a narrow-boat, although if I know Steady Ormerod you'll find him in the Golden Perch at this time of day! Anyone'll point him out to you . . ."

★　　　★　　　★　　　★

"Mr Ormerod?" The small figure sat hunched over the scrubbed table in the pub, a half pint before him.

"Never heard of 'im," he replied brusquely.

"My name's Linda Wood. I'm opening the craft shop in the village next week — if I can find someone to paint a sign for me, that is."

He looked up then. His eyes were a bright and clear china blue.

"It's young David you'll be wantin', then." He smiled suddenly. "I'll take you to see him, if'n you want?"

"That would be kind." Linda smiled back.

"I'm sorry if'n I was a bit sharp with you back there," he began as they headed up the lane. "You never can tell with folk you don't know."

Linda smiled wryly.

"Or even with folk you do, sometimes."

The narrow-boat was a picture. The roof was decked with bright flowers, the cosy interior all varnished wood and gleaming brass, and the air scented with wax polish.

Mr Ormerod led her down the companion-way into a long, narrow sitting-room.

"David! Customer for you." The old man smiled. "I'll be off, then."

WHAT was that?"
   A tall figure appeared in the far doorway, a heavy jumper halfway over his head.

"Oh, it's you." He finished pulling down the jumper.

Linda blushed. It was the man she had seen watching her in the lane that first day.

"Hilda at the shop told me that you paint signs," she said quickly. "And I need one painting."

He smiled, a warm friendly smile that lit up his rugged face.

"I do boats mostly," he said. "But I don't suppose there's that much difference."

"So you'll do it?" She felt strangely uneasy in his company. Not that she was frightened; that penetrating gaze of his just seemed to unsettle her.

"I'll come around this afternoon, if you like. You can show me what you had in mind?"

"That would be wonderful."

He seemed to approve of what they'd done with the old bakery when he arrived that afternoon.

"Will the sign take long?" Her one concern was to get the place up and running as soon as possible.

"A day or so, no more." He looked approvingly at her sketches.

"Mummy, the General's back! Come and look, quickly."

Linda smiled apologetically at her visitor, and together they crossed to the low stone wall that bounded the small garden. Emma was sitting at the edge of the neat lawn, in the middle of which sat a large cat. Quietly, Linda opened the wicket gate and stepped into the garden.

"My, he is big," she whispered.

"That's the General, all right." As David spoke the cat got up and, walking right up to him, began to rub itself against his legs.

"He knows you!" Emma cried in astonishment.

David laughed gently.

"Oh, yes, the General and I are old friends. Why not try stroking him?"

Linda watched the pleasure in his face. He talked with Emma as if they were old friends. A good, honest man, she caught herself thinking.

Tentatively, Emma reached out to touch the cat's glossy coat.

"He's all soft and warm." With sudden excitement she turned to her mother. "Can we have a cat like the General, Mummy, please?"

"We'll see once we get settled, Emma." She exchanged a rueful glance with David.

"I think I'd better get on with that sign of yours."

He came back with it two days later.

"It's wonderful! Far better than I could have imagined," Linda told him honestly.

"Well, now all we have to do is get it fixed over the door." He grinned.

Linda could see exactly what he meant. The sign was painted on a plywood base eight feet long and eighteen inches wide, and was both heavy and bulky.

"I've got two sets of step ladders. Will that help?"

Eventually they got it in position. David stood on one set of steps, holding the sign in the middle, while Linda fixed one end. Then, moving to the other end they stood side by side, one supporting while the other fixed.

David was just driving the last screw home when the foot of Linda's step ladder slipped. She lurched sideways as the flimsy aluminium collapsed beneath her, only to be checked at the last moment by an iron grip about her waist.

David had dropped the screwdriver and snatched her into his arms as she fell.

For a moment they remained motionless, their faces close together. She could smell the dry muskiness of his skin, feel his body pressed close to hers . . .

"That was close," she croaked, her heart racing.

For a moment his eyes remained locked on hers. Then he blinked, as if waking from a dream. His grip on her eased, and he let her gently to the ground.

"I think that about does it." He avoided her glance.

She sensed the sudden gulf that had opened between them, and was stung by it.

"Yes, I'm grateful for your help."

"I'll be off then," he said — and left before she could reply.

THE craft shop was a success. Linda's beautiful pots and bowls, together with the carefully selected stock she bought in, sold well. As word spread, people came from far and wide to buy her dried flowers and unusual china ornaments.

It wasn't long before she realised that the shop would indeed provide them with an income they could live on. The gamble had paid off.

She had little time to think of David during those first hectic days. Sometimes at night, as she sat beside her cosy log fire, or lay tucked up in bed, her thoughts would drift back to those heady moments in his arms. The vision of his face close to hers would steal into her thoughts at the oddest times.

He hadn't been back to the shop since that afternoon, and as the days turned into weeks she realised that she would have to visit him.

Magic Recipe

*T*HERE'S *a mixture made for
marriage,
You will find it heaven-sent!
If you realise love must always be
The main ingredient.
You will need a generous sprinkling
Of mutual tolerance,
A great big pinch of humour
And a garnish of romance.
This recipe is all you need
To keep you close together.
Some even claim it's guaranteed
To make love last for ever!*

— *Gaye Wilson.*

He hadn't sent in a bill, and no matter how awkward she might feel about meeting him again, she knew she couldn't let his efforts go unrewarded.

One Thursday morning, Linda dropped Emma off at school, placed a *Closed for stocktaking* sign in the shop window and set out along the windswept canal bank.

She knew the boat was empty even before she stepped on board. There was no smoke coming from the tiny chimney, and all the windows were in darkness.

For a few moments she stood staring out across the cold grey waters. The canal was very wide here. The far bank was a mass of reed beds that gave the place a wild, natural look.

"Watch your step. It's very deep as well as wide."

She turned suddenly at the sound of the voice — his voice.

"I didn't hear you."

He stood on the tow-path beside the stooped figure of his grandfather. The old man's eyes flicked from Linda's face to David's and back again.

"I'm goin' to take the dog for a walk."

"We don't have a dog, Grandad." David's eyes never left Linda's face.

"Light the stove before the poor girl freezes to death," Steady called over his shoulder.

David smiled then.

"Sorry. He's right. It is cold out there."

She followed him down into the boat. In minutes the stove was crackling brightly and the air became tinged with sweet wood smoke.

"Would you like some coffee?"

Linda smiled and nodded. It was as if they were both acting, she thought, to avoid real conversation. Finally she could stand it no longer. She was compelled to speak.

"Why didn't you send a bill for the sign?"

He froze, spoon poised above cup.

"It was a gift," he said finally as he poured hot water into the two mugs. He carefully stirred them and handed one to Linda.

"There's milk and sugar on the table."

"I can't let you do that. All the work you put in on that sign . . . You *must* let me pay you." She smiled gently as she poured milk into her mug.

"You'll soon be bankrupt if you do business like that." It was a casual, half-joking remark, but he flinched as if she'd slapped his face.

"I have no *business*, as you put it. Not now, not ever. What I do, I do because it suits me, and for no other reason."

Linda's cheeks burned fiercely. What had she said?

"I'm sorry if I offended you, but . . ." The words dried on her lips.

"No, it's me who should be sorry." He turned to gaze unseeingly out across the cold expanse of water.

There was a long silence between them. Finally it was Linda who spoke.

"Why is the canal so wide here?"

He looked round. Sudden understanding sparkled deep in his eyes, and he smiled.

"The land around here is part of the estate of the local lord of the manor. When the canal company wanted to push a waterway through the then earl's land, he insisted that they make it look as natural as possible — hence the wides."

"Now that's what I call power." She was watching his expression carefully.

"Money can't buy everything." He took up his mug of coffee.

Linda decided to try another tack. She wasn't going home till she'd got past the barrier he had built around himself.

"I hear your grandfather's something of a local hero."

His expression cleared. "A rather reluctant one."

He got to his feet and crossed to an old dresser. "Here, I'll show you something." He pulled out a battered leather case and handed it to her.

Nestling on deep blue velvet was a medal with a faded ribbon.

"Is it really . . .?"

Her voice was reduced to a reverent whisper.

"Yes. Grandad was in bomb disposal. 'Steady Eddy Ormerod,' they called him, because he had the steadiest hands anyone had ever seen.

"He only ever failed to defuse one bomb that he was sent out to, in the basement of a hospital. Eddy picked the thing up and carried it out of there by himself.

"He dropped it down a well at the bottom of the hospital yard, and was all but killed in the explosion. That's what they gave him the medal for."

Linda met his eyes. Her own were full of tears.

"My father told me the story," David added. "Eddy would never talk about it."

"You and your father must be very proud of him."

"My father's dead. He killed himself when his business crashed."

THE words hit her like a sledgehammer.

"Is that why you stepped out of life? Why you're frightened of becoming involved?"

Linda braced herself for the outburst, but it never came.

Finally she looked into his face. There was no anger there any more, only sadness, and a loneliness that made her heart ache.

"Is it that obvious?" he said.

"It seemed such a pity, that's all. You have a real talent. A talent that should be used, not hidden away."

"Should you be preaching about hiding away?"

Linda blushed hotly.

"I'm making a fresh start," she murmured, turning away to bite back tears.

"I'm sorry. I didn't mean to hurt you." He came closer then, his arm going around her shoulder, comfortingly.

"It's all right. I'm just being silly."

Strong fingers gently turned her face towards his. They carried a smell of linseed oil and paint.

"I don't think you're silly," he said softly. "I think you're dead right."

She looked up into his eyes, and her heart beat heavily at the expression there. He leaned forward and kissed her then, a fleeting, shy kiss.

"Perhaps we have more in common than we thought," she said huskily.

His arms tightened about her as they kissed again, passionately, eagerly this time.

"Oh! Sorry."

They sprang apart at the sound of the Wing Commander's voice. He was standing, red-faced and uneasy, at the cabin door.

"I'm sorry to barge in like this," he stammered. "Steady said I would find you here, Miss — er — Linda."

"Is there something wrong? Emma?" Linda's thoughts turned instantly to her daughter.

"It depends on how you look at it. The General has just given birth to three kittens in your garden! I heard her meowing from across the lane . . ."

David and Linda exchanged a look of astonishment, and began to laugh helplessly.

"I think we'd better get over there," David said as their laughter subsided, and Linda wiped away a tear of happiness.

"Oh, heavens!" she exclaimed. "You know what this means? Emma will want to keep the lot!" □

by OLWEN RICHARDS

WHEN Anne, who owned the hairdressing salon, decided to retire to full-time motherhood, I didn't lose a wink of sleep. "Making Waves" was such a flourishing concern that somebody was sure to snap it up.

Our regulars expressed concern, of course, because it was the only salon in the area, our nearest rival being in town, over twenty miles away. Which was precisely why, I hastened to assure them, it made a perfect little business proposition.

But six months on, we'd not had one inquiry. If I could have raised the cash, I would have taken it myself, but I had to stand by helplessly as "Making Waves" went up for auction.

In the end, the next-door grocer bought the place to extend his shop and make a mini market, leaving me without a job and many of our clients in the lurch.

Which gave me an idea. I took an ad in the local paper, had a few cards printed up and put the word out on the village grapevine. "Miles of Styles" would bring my expertise directly to the comfort of the home.

I was back in business, enjoying cosy little chats and coffee with my former clients. Just like before, but better, because now they were completely at their ease and they took me into their confidence. They started to become friends.

The oldest friend, in every sense, was Mrs Parry — Elizabeth. I never could find out her age.

"My secret," she would joke. "Same as *your* secret's how to keep me looking even younger than I feel!"

Miles of Styles!

She'd always ask for the season's newest shape. It was fun to have a challenge, and I loved to practise on such gloriously soft hair.

She lived a distance from the shops, so I used to do some bits of shopping on my way. Not groceries or knitting wool for her. No, Elizabeth would send me for the latest skin-care products and cosmetics.

For someone who was certainly on the other side of seventy, she had an admirable zest for life.

She worked long hours in her garden, rising at the crack of dawn. The house was overflowing with her flowers, and if you'd peeped into her pantry you'd have been knocked out. Rows and rows of jars and bottles. Jams and chutneys, scented vinegars and oils, as well as wines and cordials, all made from fruit and herbs she grew.

You can imagine my dismay when, arriving after lunch one summer's day, I found the milk still on the doorstep and the curtains drawn. Knocking raised no answer, so I called her name.

Luckily, she'd never paid a bit of notice to my warnings about security. The key to Toptree Cottage was still underneath a stone by her back step. I let myself into the kitchen, and found her in a crumpled heap beside the cooker, conscious but dazed with pain.

"I fell last night," she whispered, as I tried to comfort her. "My stupid leg . . ."

I wrapped my jacket round her.

"I'll get an ambulance."

Elizabeth was propped against a pile of hospital pillows when I visited the ward that evening. It saddened me to see how suddenly the hale and hearty woman I knew had been transformed into a frail old lady. But her pale face lit up on seeing me.

"I should know better at my age than to go standing on a stool!" She smiled wryly. "Won't be standing on anything now for quite a while." She pointed to the cage above her legs.

"I've rung your daughter," I said, trying to sound cheery as I took her hand. "She'll come at the weekend."

"It's such a long way, and her with children of her own. I'm just a nuisance."

"Rubbish!" I declared. "You've never bothered anyone."

"I used to like my independence."

"You will again, Elizabeth, as soon as that leg is mended. Meanwhile lie back and try to take it easy. I've brought you grapes and squash and magazines . . ."

She squeezed my hand.

"You make it seem like a holiday!"

"Not quite a luxury hotel, but I can guarantee the guests are well looked after! Now, is there any more that I can do?"

Her forehead wrinkled.

"I'd love it if you'd comb my hair. And," she hesitated, "if you've got a touch of lipstick on you . . .?"

"Spoken like the true Elizabeth! Mine isn't quite your colour, though. Would you like me to pop home and fetch yours?"

She nodded gratefully.

"If you'd check around, see everything's all right . . . You've got the spare key still?"

EDZELL, ANGUS

THIS pretty village lies in the foothills of the Grampian mountains north of Brechin. Approaching from the south, the road runs under the Dalhousie arch. Edzell Castle dates from mediaeval times, and these days is known for the beauty of its walled garden, which has box hedges clipped into the words and symbols of the Lindsay coat of arms. The "lichtsome" Lindsays acquired the village and estate about 1375.

EDZELL, ANGUS : J CAMPBELL KERR

NEXT morning, with an hour between appointments, I made my way up to the cottage. Opening the back door, I stepped inside and froze. The usually tidy room was in a state of total chaos. It simply wasn't possible! All those years Elizabeth had kept a key outside, and the first night it was gone, she had been burgled!

As I gazed around, it dawned on me that there was something very odd about this break-in. Thieves took stuff away. They didn't add a pile of mugs and tinfoil dishes to the table, or fill the sink close to overflowing . . .

"And who might you be?" a voice behind me said.

I jumped and looked around. A man stood in the doorway, glowering at me.

"Lynn," I blurted, trying not to sound frightened. "Lynn Walters. I'm the hairdresser. I found Elizabeth . . ."

My shaky voice dwindled into silence.

"Ah!" he said, extending his right hand. "Mark Andrews. I'm her grandson."

My eyes grew wider.

"You're the little angel in the photo on the mantelpiece?" I said slowly.

"Not so little, or angelic any more." He grinned. "And not domesticated, either. Mum sent me up here to keep the cottage safe till she arrived herself, but I'm afraid I've made a dreadful mess already.

"You see, I stopped off last night and got a take-away, but then I was too tired to wash up. I scraped the remnants down the sink, forgetting Gran's not got a waste disposal unit. I didn't realise the stuff would set like concrete overnight . . ."

We gazed in solemn silence at the stagnant water in the sink.

"It's almost running over," I remarked unnecessarily.

"Salvation is at hand. I've found the rubber plunger thing."

"All yours," I said, stepping back hastily.

★   ★   ★   ★

There was a sort of panic in Elizabeth's eyes when I told her about Mark, and I hadn't even mentioned her wrecked kitchen.

"He isn't housetrained, Lynn. I was expecting to be there when he came up next week . . ."

"You didn't say."

"Well, that's how I came to have the accident. I'd put the letter behind the clock, and I was trying to get it down again. He's had promotion," she said proudly. "He'll be moving up here to work and he plans to stay with me until he finds a flat. Mark's really very clever, but he isn't practical at all."

I nodded sympathetically and said nothing.

"I do wish his mother had left well alone," Elizabeth said peevishly.

"He's busy settling in," I answered non-committally. "He'll be along tonight to visit. I've got your make-up, if you'd like me to apply a touch of glamour for his benefit."

She gave an anxious smile.

"I don't suppose . . ." She paused, and sighed. "I couldn't put you to the bother."

"What?" I coaxed.

"Well, if you could drop by? Not specially, just when you happen to be passing. To keep an eye on Toptree . . ."

Toptree wasn't actually on my way to anywhere, but Elizabeth was a dear friend and Mark was such a clot. How could I refuse?

YOU didn't tell her?" Mark asked anxiously, emerging from beneath the sink.

"As if I would. She's in enough pain as it is."

"Thank heavens. That you didn't tell, I mean."

"It doesn't guarantee I won't if you don't get the kitchen sorted sharpish."

"No problem, Lynn." He grinned. "The sink is working fine . . . I think."

"Terrific! You've a stack of washing-up to practise with."

Mark gazed around and groaned.

"I'm never going to get through before it's time to visit Gran. I don't suppose," he continued, with a beguiling smile, "you'd . . ."

"No!" I answered firmly. But then he smiled again . . .

"I owe you dinner at the very least," he said, when I had put the last few plates away and hung my teacloth up to dry. "Do you have a favourite restaurant?"

For a moment I was tempted. The prospect of somebody willing to foot the bill at Luigi's had great appeal. Especially somebody with considerable charm. And Mark had lots of that. You'd not have found me tackling that mess unless he had been the kind who could have lured birds from trees.

I steeled myself, and shook my head.

"We'd better come straight back from the hospital. You've got a lot to learn before Elizabeth's discharged, if you don't want to drive her mad."

He pulled a face, although his eyes were twinkling slightly.

"But Gran loves looking after me! She would feel cheated if I could manage on my own."

"Listen, Mark," I said grimly. "Your gran is a marvel for her age, but in reality she's an old lady. She's the one who's going to need looking after when she finally comes home."

He got the message, especially when he first saw Elizabeth in that white bed. Clearly they loved each other to distraction, and he got quite a shock to see how frail she looked.

The pasta we ate that evening was a molten mess beneath a very chewy sauce. However, Mark was really proud of it. I washed it down with wine and tried to sound encouraging.

"At least," he pointed out, "I didn't block the sink."

In fact, he never blocked the sink again. By the time Elizabeth got home, he'd mastered spaghetti, and a whole lot more.

"I don't know what you've done to him," Elizabeth said to me, "but he's a different man!"

"I've not done anything," I murmured innocently.

Mark winked at me behind her back and blew a kiss.

Three months later, Mark moved out of Elizabeth's again, into a flat in town. I went round to help him learn new dishes, which really seemed quite often.

Then came the moment I was dreading — the day my repertoire ran out. We had washed up and slumped on to the sofa with our coffee, like we always did. Like we'd never do again unless we could find an excuse . . . I swallowed hard.

"I think," I blurted out unhappily, "I've taught you all I can."

There was a brief but hideous silence.

"I wouldn't go as far as that." Mark slid his arm around my waist and pulled me close. "There's life beyond the kitchen stove, after all."

"There is?" I whispered, lifting up my face to meet the melting kiss I'd somehow given up expecting.

"I meant to tell you long ago," he said, when he could, "but there were always saucepans in the way."

"They're safely stacked away tonight!"

It was a lot later, when we got around to heating up the coffee, that he handed me the parcel.

"A Culinary A to Z — all you'll ever need to know!" I looked puzzled.

"Should last a lifetime," Mark said. "Of course, we'll have to start at the beginning. I've marked one page in 'A' I thought might be of special interest. Just there, where you can see the lump . . ."

It was an amethyst set in soft rose gold.

"Heirloom," Mark confided, slipping it on to my finger. "Gran's thrilled I'm giving it to you. She says you've an eye for beauty, and she understands these things."

"I'll treasure it for both of you," I murmured, gazing at my delicate antique engagement ring.

I wore the ring all the time, except when we were cooking, and, though we didn't make much headway, that book provided us with hours of fun. But nothing lasts for ever.

Eighteen months ago, halfway through the "B"s, Elizabeth conceded Toptree Cottage was too much for her and she decided to accept her daughter's offer of a home.

Mark moved back to Toptree then, and everything became more serious.

We've had to skip to "S" for speedy snacks, because we haven't got the time nowadays. We have to cater for another, much more choosy eater. "Miles of Styles" has taken on a sleeping partner, when I'm lucky. Oftener than not, however, she's giggling and cooing at my clients, or wailing for a change of nappy at the crucial moment of a perm.

But no-one seems to mind at all. Why, only yesterday, the scratchiest of my ladies, stroking my daughter's pink cheeks, suggested I re-name the business "Miles of Smiles." □

The Blossoming Of Lily

AS headmistress of Meredith High School for Girls, I was duty-bound to wear a hat for important occasions. I had a felt cloche for Founder's Day and a navy straw for the summer prizegiving.

During the first week of my retirement I donated them to the church jumble sale. I haven't worn a hat since.

Then Jilly, my only granddaughter, decided to get married.

"As grandmother of the bride, you've *got* to have a hat!" she insisted. "Mum's bought a super one to match her outfit and Jim's mother and grandmother are off shopping next Saturday . . ."

"You're not expecting me to compete with Jim's gran, are you?" I protested. "She was a child bride — and I was a late starter. I'm old enough to be a great-great gran!"

"Well, you don't look it," Jilly assured me loyally. "That new shop in town has some awfully pretty hats. Why don't I come with you and help you choose?"

And that was how I allowed myself to be bullied into going to the new milliner's.

**by
MARION
TOWNSEND**

"Isn't it lovely?" Jill enthused. "The whole row of shops has a preservation order on it. You probably remember . . . ?"

I nodded. The shops were too prettified for authenticity, but I certainly recognised them. In fact, *Headlines* — Jill's new hat shop — had been a milliner's when I was a girl. Only it was called *Poppy's* then . . .

The same little bell tinkled merrily as I stepped over the threshold . . .

I wasn't prepared for the deep pile of the carpet and stumbled. The proprietor stepped forward quickly and clutched my arm.

"Are you OK, Gran?" Jilly asked anxiously.

"Yes." I made the mistake of trying to explain. "I was just expecting to step on to lino . . ."

This remark did little to reassure Jilly. And the proprietor was obviously thinking I was a doddery old woman, unlikely to be able to afford a hat.

"I'm perfectly all right!" I shook off the clutching arm. "I'm not in my dotage yet!"

My voice wasn't as authoritative as it had once been, but it did the trick.

Jilly gave me a sly wink and explained what we wanted.

"I'm sure we'll find something suitable." The proprietor waved her elegant, pink varnished nails at a gloomy assortment of black, grey, brown and navy felt hats. The head-hugging, hair-flattening designs were trimmed with muted braids, small neat bows or faded silk flowers.

I sighed as I trudged through the deep-pile carpet towards them. Then I saw *the* hat . . .

It sat in solitary splendour on a stand. So pretty — finely-woven black straw, with a wide, slightly turned-up brim in which grew a profusion of flamboyant silk poppies.

Totally unsuitable, of course. The wedding is in November and I'd just bought a warm, serviceable, navy-blue woollen suit. Huge-brimmed straws with bright red poppies are for the summer.

I stood in front of the mirror and put the straw hat on. My green eyes, deepset in their etchings of wrinkles, sparkled wickedly back at me from under the black rim.

"So it doesn't go with your suit?" From out of the past, Poppy's warm, chuckling voice called out to me. "Get another outfit. It might rain? Buy a red umbrella to match the poppies. Go on, I dare you . . ."

"I'll take this one." They both gaped at me open-mouthed.

Jilly flicked the price ticket over.

"It's horrendously expensive!" she whispered in my ear. "Are you sure, Gran?"

I nodded. I'd have to explain my reasons later, but first I'd have to sit down.

Sinking thankfully into the peach velvet of the only chair in the shop, I was immediately back in the past . . .

The Blossoming Of Lily

NERVOUS and shivering, I perched uncomfortably on the very edge of a high-backed wooden chair. Carefully I chanted the words my mother had made me rehearse earlier that morning . . .

"Please ma'am, I've brought samples of the very fine straw plaiting made by my mother and sisters.

"At present they sell it cheaply to a buyer from a big straw-hat factory in Luton. Ma . . . er . . . my mother was wanting to . . . er . . . cut out the middleman, like. She's heard that you make straw hats here and wondered if you'd buy the plaiting direct from us."

Relieved at having delivered Ma's message correctly, I studied Madam Poppy. How appropriate her name was!

She was wearing a swirling, silky dress in poppy-red and her violet eyes were fringed with long, black lashes. Just like the deep purple-black centre of a field poppy . . .

But was Poppy her real name? She was something of a mystery woman — a newcomer who seemed reluctant to reveal anything of her past to the town gossips.

"You look starved, you poor little thing!" she exclaimed. "What can your mother be thinking of sending you out on a day like this? Surely you should be at school by now?"

"I ain't starved, ma'am. I had porridge and bread and dripping for breakfast."

"I didn't mean hungry-starved." She gave a low, throaty chuckle. "I meant cold-starved. I come from the North, where the word serves two purposes."

"I ain't cold either," I protested. "Our May has just got a new coat, so I've got her old one and it's real cosy. But I *shall* be late for school, if . . ."

"Why didn't your mother come and see me herself? Or your sister? Are you the youngest?"

"Yes." I nodded. "I'm Lily. I ain't much of a hand at straw-plaitin', so Ma's made me the gofer.

"I go for the rush for matting and canes for caning and chair seat frames for both. Our George has made me a little cart for collecting. Ma and my sisters can't spare time to come because they've got rush orders and . . ."

"Rush-rush orders, eh?" she teased, and again she gave that gurgling laugh. "It seems to me you're a very resourceful family. These plaiting samples are excellent. I shall visit your mother this evening to negotiate a rate."

She handed me a slip of paper.

"Now write your address down and run along to school."

I galloped speedily through the back streets, told my mother the good news, then went on to school. I was half an hour late already. I was sorry and angry because I hated to miss one precious minute.

I was always happy within the four-square red-brick walls. At school I felt confident and grown-up, as I worked my way through the tasks set by Miss Frank.

"A scholarship girl if ever I saw one!" Miss Franks would mutter to herself.

I delighted in a row of ticks on the pages of difficult sums, or a high mark for my English composition. I didn't care if the other children teased me and called me teacher's pet, or sniggered when Miss Frank gave me a book to take home and read.

Ma didn't approve of book-learning and talk of scholarships.

"How does she think I can afford your books and uniform if you win a place to that posh High School?

"You're a dreamer like your pa — and look where dreaming has got him! A clever wheelwright, he doesn't care for hard work, does he? Stuffs himself with book nonsense and wants to go adventuring!"

I often wondered why my parents got married. They were so different.

A beloved only child, born late to elderly parents, staunch chapel-goers and fervent members of the Temperance movement, my mother had a strict country upbringing. My father's parents were all devil-may-care, back-street town folk with a weakness for alcohol, which my father inherited.

My mother still yearned for her country origins, and she'd picked pretty, floral names for us girls. There were May, Iris, Rose, Violet, and me — Lily.

My brother couldn't be named for a flower! He was given a herbal name — Basil. Not surprisingly, he preferred to be called by his second name, George.

My mother's name was Mary, so one of Father's regular taunts

Summer Remembered

WHEN days are dark,
* I think awhile*
Of summer's gold on strath and
*   stream,*
Where stony tracks my steps beguile
* To heights where silver lochans*
*   gleam.*

I think of rowan trees in bloom,
* Of silken sands by soft waves kissed,*
Of moors ablaze with gorse and broom,
* And mountains crowned with*
*   mist.*

Of harebells dancing in the sun,
* And shadow-patterns on the brae,*
And colours melting, one by one,
* To moonlight at the close of day.*

Of toadstools bright on forest floors,
* And sunlit trails beneath the trees,*
And drifts of shells on golden shores,
* And songs of waterfalls. All these*
Remembered beauties play their part,
On winter days, to lift the heart.

— Brenda G. Macrow.

was, "Well, Mary, how does your garden grow? Are our little flowers blooming? A blooming nuisance, eh?"

And then he would turn to my brother. "Isn't it time our Basil found a sweetheart called Rosemary and set up his own little herb garden?"

The jokes about our flower names ceased abruptly soon after my ninth birthday. My father, without a word to anyone, disappeared, never to return.

"Well, at least there'll not be any more little flowers to add to our family garden!" May pointed out.

Iris blushed, giggled and then pointed to me. "Small pitchers have big ears."

I remember feeling annoyed. In spite of my ability to read long words in Miss Franks's books, my family often spoke a language I couldn't understand.

And this set me wondering why I seemed to be such an odd one out at home. They told me that I was "the clever one," yet I watched enviously as my sisters' nimble fingers wove rushes for matting or sent bobbins dancing merrily to make pillow lace.

I was always all fingers and thumbs, so was only trusted with fetching the raw materials and returning the finished goods. Oh, and I'd go to the market for cheap scrag ends of meat, bruised vegetables and over-ripe fruit, so Ma could concoct tasty meals to fill our hungry stomachs.

Our George refused to help me with blackberry picking, but he did come to pick crab-apples, walnuts and hazelnuts. As the weather got colder, he helped me trundle the cart to the nearest woodland to collect fallen branches.

Then George found a sweetheart . . .

I was the only one in the family who didn't take to Ivy. Maybe I was jealous, because I'd always tagged along after George until she came along.

She was well named — a coy, clinging girl, who hung on George's arm and stared adoringly into his eyes. She had a high-pitched giggle and no opinions of her own at all.

I realised later that it was because Ivy agreed with everything my mother said, that she became a favourite. She soon joined our family sweatshop and, I had to admit, worked as skilfully as my sisters.

WHEN Poppy knocked at the door to negotiate terms for the straw plaiting, everything began to go wrong.

My mother, sisters and Ivy were busy on an urgent order for pillow lace that evening. They were perched on the high-backed wooden chairs, all wearing white, starched, cotton pinnies to keep the delicate work clean.

As I ushered Poppy into the parlour, they looked up, their beaded bobbins and busy tongues stilled as they stared wide-eyed at the glowing creature, in her swirling gown of bright red silk.

I was furious that Mother didn't let me listen to the negotiations. I was stamping about and rattling crockery in the kitchen, where I'd been sent to make tea, when George returned from work.

Hissing like the steaming kettle, I explained what was going on. George offered to help me take the loaded tea-tray into the parlour.

"You're just being nosy," I teased.

I was glad I was carrying the tray with the best tea-set. George had the cake, and nearly dropped it when he saw Poppy. He stood there, mouth open, the plate tilting, until May snatched it from him.

As Ma made the introductions, George and Poppy stared at each other. Ivy, usually slow on the uptake, realised the other woman was a rival. She jumped up to hang on George's arm possessively.

Over tea, Poppy explained she had been planning to convert an old shed at the rear of her shop into a straw-plaiting work-shed. My visit, she told me with a warm smile, had come just as she'd saved the necessary money.

She'd asked a reliable local builder to undertake the conversion and, when it had been completed, she hoped to employ all my sisters. They'd undertake various types of straw-plaiting at first and then, those who showed an aptitude would make up the hats.

"I would hope to keep you all fully employed, then your clever little Lily can concentrate on her schoolwork."

"I'd be happy to do odd jobs for you, ma'am," I offered eagerly. I already adored the vivacious Poppy.

"Plenty of work round here, my girl, if your sisters are out working," my mother snapped.

The Blossoming Of Lily

MY sisters thoroughly enjoyed their new-found freedom. Poppy encouraged them to model her hats, and, for the first time in their lives, they attended chapel socials, concerts and plays and even dances in the town hall.

There was also a change in my brother. From the first time he'd stared into Poppy's violet eyes, he seemed to grow from a gangling youth into a handsome man. He was suddenly taller, broader, more mature and confident. There was a jut to his chin, a twinkle in his dark brown eyes, a swagger in his walk.

My mother had introduced him to Poppy as George. To our surprise, he'd smiled, straightened his shoulders, and confessed that his first name was Basil. The family called him George, he said, but his friends had nicknamed him "Baz."

We all gaped open-mouthed. We hadn't known that!

From that day, everyone started calling him Baz — except Ivy. And she stubbornly refused to work for Poppy, implying with a sneer that she preferred a more genteel occupation than working in a factory!

But she would continue with the lace-making orders, she said. My mother, stunned by Poppy's take-over, was delighted to have someone to gossip with.

I think Ivy felt that, if George saw her regularly, she'd win him back.

But I knew that Ivy had lost. George didn't exist any more. He had become Baz — handsome, suave and confident, peacock-proud to be walking out with Poppy.

At first, my mother was grateful to Poppy. Then the sarcastic comments began . . .

"I dunno as we've done the right thing. All you girls beholden to her for your wages. She's the sort that's likely to disappear, just like your pa did!

"And where did she come from, I'd like to know? How did she get all that money for that workshop?"

"Poppy told us she came from up North. She saved the money from her profits," I pointed out.

"And how did she afford the shop in the first place? No better than she ought to be . . . And as for Poppy, what sort of name is that?"

"It's a flower name — same as ours," May pointed out tartly.

"Poppy's a good, kind lady," Rose said, stepping forward to stand beside May.

I joined my sisters and added my two-pennyworth.

"She goes to church every Sunday and sings in the choir. The vicar's asked her to do solos."

"Well, of course she likes singing! 'Tis a chance for her to show off. Ivy reckons that, by wearing a different hat every week, your precious Mad Hatter has found a cheap way to advertise her wares!"

With that nasty innuendo Ma, as usual, had the last word.

We girls exchanged knowing glances. We were sure Ivy was behind this. We'd nick-named her Poison Ivy and sang Poppy's praises at every opportunity.

IT was a brief blossoming for Ma's flower girls. Suddenly, splitting our lives asunder as sharply as the frail straws were split for plaiting, came the Great War.

My brother was one of the first to answer the beckoning finger on the posters proclaiming *Your Country Needs You!*

My sisters were next to respond to the call. As tin hats came into fashion, they became "munition" girls at one of the local factories.

Even Ivy abandoned her genteel lace-work. She went to work in a factory which made the elm cases and canvas slings which attached bombs to those new-fangled aircraft.

Poppy closed both shop and work-shed and volunteered to be an ambulance driver in France. We heard nothing from her for those first two dreadful years.

We were all afraid for Baz, who was flying one of the first flimsy planes.

My mother blamed Poppy for this. She felt if he'd still been quiet, immature George, he would have been content to be a soldier in the infantry.

We pointed out that infantrymen were in just as much danger from bullets and shells as our Baz was high up in the sky.

In 1916, Baz and Poppy came home on leave together. How they wangled it we didn't know. They wouldn't say anything about the war, but their gaunt, pale faces and haunted eyes told us more than words.

Poppy wore a diamond engagement ring — but told us she wouldn't get a wedding ring until after the war. If God spared them both . . .

In the meantime, they made the most of their few precious days together. They just wanted to be left alone, wandering the fields and woods which seemed so green and peaceful.

We waved them a tearful goodbye on the station, wondering if we'd see either of them again.

But, within a few months, Poppy was back. Apparently, there was

CANTERBURY

MORE than 2000 years old, Canterbury was the centre from which St Augustine began his mission in 597 to spread Christianity in England. Today, Canterbury Cathedral is the Mother Church of the Anglican communion. About half of the mediaeval walls remain, and they themselves were built on Roman foundations. The West Gate, one of the original seven gates, guarded the entrance to the city from the London direction. It still stands and is now a museum.

OLD WEAVERS' HOUSE, CANTERBURY : J CAMPBELL KERR

a shortage of horses so a few of the ambulance drivers had been allowed home.

By then I was eleven years old and was working beside Ivy. I felt miserable and imprisoned in that huge, dark factory, but I did my poor best to sew the strips of canvas.

Ivy helped me, undoing and finishing my clumsy efforts without the foreman noticing.

"Must make 'em good and strong, Lily. They might be slung under George's airyplane. Don't want them falling out, do we?"

On my third day Poppy swept to the rescue. I was almost in tears, staring down at my hands, which were rubbed raw from the canvas. Ivy nudged me.

"What's the Mad Hatter doin' here, Lily?"

I looked up. Poppy, resplendent in purple, swept towards our bench, her high heels clicking on the wooden floor. The hem of her skirt swished aside the offcuts of elm, sawdust and canvas and the tiny foreman followed, protesting loudly.

"You can't come in here, madam. We're on secret war work."

Poppy ignored him.

"Lily!" she announced in her clear, commanding voice. "Get your coat and come with me. You're going back to school!"

"The girl is employed here legitimately," the foreman hissed. "She passed the special leaving exam."

Poppy whirled round to face him.

"You should have refused to take her on. She's only eleven. Surely we haven't let this war put us back to the dark ages of sweatshops and child labour!"

"Oh, no, madam. But . . . well the rules have been somewhat relaxed. The youngsters are on reduced hours and the work is not too arduous . . ."

Poppy was still arguing with him when I got back with my coat.

"Hurry, Lily," she said, taking my arm.

"What will her mother say?" Ivy spoke for the first time.

"I've talked to Lily's mother already." Poppy glared at her scornfully. "She's agreed that, war or no war, Lily is to stay on at school.

"Her teacher assures me she will win a scholarship place. We need more women with a good education. Maybe if women had more say-so in running the world there would be no more wars . . ."

She paused, tears trembling on her dark lashes. Then she reached forward and touched Ivy's hand.

"If you could see it! Oh, Ivy, pray for him . . . your George . . . my Baz . . . and for all the other poor souls . . ."

JILLY was waiting for her new husband at the hall door to greet their wedding reception guests. She stepped forward to give me a hug and knocked my hat sideways.

She giggled and stretched up to set it straight.

"Gran!" She gasped in surprise. "You've lost your poppies! They must have fallen off.

Part 3

AS darkness fell at Prestonpans, the two armies camped out with a treacherous marsh between them. Then a local man, a Jacobite supporter, offered to lead the Prince's army safely through the marshes, so that they could take the army of Sir John Cope by surprise.

The ruse worked well. The Government troops were quite unprepared, and the Highlanders made short work of them. That well-known derisory song sums it up —

"Hey, Johnny Cope are ye waukin yet."

From Prestonpans the Highland army moved southwards towards Edinburgh and ever nearer the English Border.

The Prince himself made a halt at Traquair (near Peebles) the home of the Earl of Traquair, a staunch Jacobite and old friend of his father.

Traquair can claim to be the oldest inhabited mansion-house in Scotland, and a thousand years of history lie behind those grey walls. The Prince duly admired the famous Bear Gates leading to the main avenue, and revelled in all the Royal associations. He was especially pleased when presented with an "Amen" glass with a toast to himself engraved upon it.

Alas, how was he to know that within a few months he and his army would pass Traquair again — in full retreat?

The Earl Of Traquair ordered the Bear Gates to be closed, and never opened again until a Stuart was once more on the throne.

"Whose car did you come in? Really — that hat was so expensive! You'd think the trimmings would be fixed better!"

"It was me," I confessed. "I snipped them off with my manicure scissors.

"You know the war memorial is in the church grounds? Well, my poppies are there. It's Remembrance Day tomorrow. They're in memory of Poppy."

"You mean the one you told me about? The lovely Mad Hatter? Was she killed?"

"Yes." I blinked back my tears. "Driving her ambulance towards the front line.

"Her name isn't on the Roll of Honour. Only the servicemen. Your Uncle Baz's name's there, of course. He survived the First War only to get killed in the Battle of Britain.

"He never got over Poppy, you know. He stayed in the service . . . first the RFC, then the RAF . . . Poor Ivy. She had to settle for a curate. Made him a lovely prim and proper wife!"

Jilly smiled at me and patted my arm.

"It was a lovely thought, Gran. Poppies for a brave Poppy!"

Wiping away my tears with a small lace hankie, I walked away from the happy couple to find my seat next to Jim's gran.

There would be a few surprised faces tomorrow at the war memorial. Those flamboyant poppies had flaunted themselves over the cold stone. How Poppy would have appreciated them! □

E

BARBARA was glad Jenny had bullied her into buying the rose-pink dress, now that seventy pairs of eyes were watching her.

She could remember how she'd protested. "I can't afford it — and it's too young for me."

"It's not," her daughter had told her. "It's perfect, and you look great in it. Now all we've got to do is get you a hat to go with it!"

So she'd let Jenny have her way, and the result, as she'd seen in her bedroom mirror this morning, had been worth every penny.

For Better Or For Worse

by
PAT
FREER

Knowing she looked her best, she'd walked composedly past all the assembled guests and arranged herself in the left-hand pew. Graciously, she'd nodded and smiled at Adam and his parents in the pews opposite.

Once seated, listening to the organ, she was very conscious of being alone. Well, she'd better get used to that, now that Jenny was leaving home for good!

But did you ever get used to it? Perhaps not. Perhaps being the odd one out in a world of couples would always remain painful. Barbara had been widowed two years ago, and the ache was lessening, but she was still irritated by the would-be helpfuls, who mouthed platitudes.

"Time is a great healer, Barbara. You're still young enough to start again."

She'd longed to tell them to be quiet, but of course she didn't. They were only trying to be kind. They didn't understand.

George had been a wonderful husband, and a good stepfather to Jenny, but seven years together hadn't been enough. It was even less than the twelve years Barbara had been married to Jack, Jenny's father. If only George had been here today, to give Jenny away.

The sound of the organ changed as it began on the crashing chords of Mendelssohn's wedding march. Behind her, there was a muttering and a rustling as people craned their necks to look back at the church entrance.

Adam stepped forward. He gave Barbara a grin, before turning very deliberately sideways and gazing up the aisle. He'd warned Jenny that he was going to watch her walk to him as his bride.

"It's the only time in my life I'll get the chance," he'd said. "I'm not taking my eyes off you."

Hadn't someone said something like that before?

A memory stirred. Twenty-four years ago she, too, had come down an aisle, wearing the same dress Jenny was wearing today. Jack had watched her all the way, his dark eyes warm, loving and admiring.

Fleetingly, she remembered the bitterness, the emptiness, when he'd left . . . but it was all so long ago now, so long ago it didn't matter any more.

Jenny came closer . . . to Barbara's annoyance, her daughter was just a misty blur. The tears she'd been afraid of had come.

She took a tissue out of her bag. It worked well on her brimming eyes, but was powerless to stem the flood of recollections.

Jenny, a happy, fat, pink baby, gurgling and laughing in her pram. Jenny on her first day at school, her hair in bunches.

Then the child had changed into a bubbly, healthy teenager — and, finally, into the beautiful woman she now was.

Oh, how I'll miss you, Jenny!

The mist had cleared. Jenny was just yards away.

But the man beside her wasn't her uncle! It was — it was — a stranger? Yet . . . not a stranger . . .

Barbara drew in her breath sharply. The tall, tanned, formally-suited figure upon whose arm her daughter's hand rested was — no, it couldn't be. Jenny wouldn't do this to her. Not without telling her!

But she had. It was Jack. Jenny's father.

He was looking straight at her, a quizzical, inquiring look. So was Jenny. There was apology in both those looks.

Forgive me, Mum. I'll explain later, Jenny's eyes told her, before they flew back to her bridegroom.

Jack's dark eyes had a different message. They, too, asked for forgiveness, but there was something else, too. Something appreciative . . . a little alarming . . .

Jenny, you'd better have a good explanation for this, Barbara thought. Her hard-won tranquillity was almost gone.

She hardly heard the minister after the opening words.

"Dearly beloved. We are gathered together . . . to join this man and this woman."

THE years slipped away. She was a girl again, hearing those words for the first time. Her heart lurched, remembering. She and Jack had been so in love, so young, so eager . . .

Was he remembering, too? She studied the upright back. He was still attractive even at fifty, she decided, with a sneaky little feeling of pride. Maturity had made him more distinguished.

The curly hair at the back of his neck was grey. Momentarily, she mourned for the black gloss of his youth, then registered the fact that the hair was too long. It curled over his collar.

Jack had never remarried, but Barbara had heard he'd had a long-term girlfriend. She was glad for him. She hoped he was happy . . .

"Who gives this woman . . . ?"

Jack took up Jenny's left hand and exchanged a look with his daughter that gave Barbara's heart another twist.

Those annual trips to the United States that Jenny had made, to stay with her father, had hurt Barbara at first. Eventually, she'd grown used to them and, after a while, they'd become routine.

She'd never asked about anything and Jenny had been strangely reticent. Today, for the first time, Barbara realised she hadn't wanted to see, or acknowledge, the bond between father and daughter.

Later, George had come into her life. They'd married and he'd been such a good stepfather. She'd had a happy family again.

For the first time she found herself wondering how Jack had felt about another man playing father to Jenny . . .

Planning the wedding, Jenny had seemed matter-of-fact.

"It has to be in May, because Adam's taking his holiday then. Dad's in Africa on a business trip for three months. Shall I ask Uncle Al to give me away?"

Barbara had been secretly relieved, glad she could feel relaxed about the ceremony and reception. She was suddenly ashamed that never once had it crossed her mind to wonder how Jack felt about missing the wedding.

ONCE his part in the ceremony was over, Jack took a step back into the pew beside her.

Acutely aware of his closeness, and how the two of them looked, side by side, to seventy interested spectators, Barbara did not raise her eyes to look at him. The big hat helped, but she knew he was looking at her, waiting for her to turn to face him.

She'd forgotten how tall he was. She only came a little higher than his shoulder. And he still smelt of the same aftershave he'd always used.

Jack always had been a creature of habit. Once he'd decided on something, he liked to stay with it. As he had her — and their marriage.

When had it all become too much? Jenny's eighth birthday party? That had been the last straw . . .

After promising to come straight home, he'd missed it. He'd been entertaining a client and arrived home, drunk, as the other children and their parents were leaving.

Jenny had cried, and Barbara had known she couldn't take any more. There'd been too many broken promises . . . too many times he'd said, "I swear it'll never happen again." She didn't want to hear the disappointment in Jenny's voice, or see the bewilderment in her face, even one more time.

So she'd made her plans and, while he slept, she packed his cases.

He woke to black coffee and an ultimatum.

"I want you to leave, Jack. We can't go on like this."

He'd tried to laugh it off, convinced it was just another threat.

"One more chance, Barbs. Just one more." He'd tried to take her in his arms and wheedle her out of it.

"Not this time, Jack." He'd finally heard the new determination in her voice, but still didn't give up.

In the past, there would have been another scene — dreadful, tearing, wrenching words as they'd both lost their tempers. But not that time. That had been different. Barbara didn't argue, she'd stayed calm, cold and distant.

"How will you manage, if I go?" Jack had asked.

"I'll go back to teaching."

"I still love you." By then, the knowledge that she meant what she said had got through to him. His dark eyes were haunted.

For one moment she'd almost weakened. Over the lump in her throat, she'd said, "I still love you, too. But I can't go on living as we are. I'm sorry, Jack. Maybe in a year or so —"

He'd left next day and she hadn't seen him since.

He'd sold the business and opened a travel agency in California. The divorce had come through and Barbara had been a single parent for the next three years.

Then she'd met George, and everything had changed . . .

At first, she'd worried every time she'd put Jenny on a plane to go and stay with her father. But Jack had been scrupulous about telling Jenny to ring to say she'd arrived safely. It had always been all right

My Grandpa Said

MY grandpa said he used to have
Thick hair upon his head,
And it was black and curly.
Well, that's what Grandpa said.

My hair is black and curly
Like Grandpa's used to be.
Do you think what happened to
Grandpa
Could one day happen to me?

— Helen Russell.

— as far as she knew!

Of course, it had meant he and Barbara had spoken on the phone — difficult, stilted conversations.

"Are you OK?"

"Yes, I'm fine — and you?"

Once Jenny was old enough to take care of her travel details for herself, even that slender contact had ceased.

THE bride and groom were moving away to sign the register. Maintaining her dignity, Barbara put her fingers on the crook of the arm Jack gallantly offered her. He smiled warmly down at her, unaware of their audience.

Hesitantly at first, she smiled back. Idiotically, the words of an old song, the one they'd called *their* song came back to her.

Getting to know you — getting to know all about you. Getting to know you — getting to love you, too.

She didn't need to get to know Jack. She knew all about him already — even if some of it was a little rusty!

Adam's parents, walking behind them, were looking at Jack curiously. Once out of sight of the congregation, Barbara introduced them.

Jack shook hands with both of them and his new son-in-law. There was bustle and chat, drowned by the sound of the still-playing organ.

Jenny came to her and hugged her.

"I'm sorry," she whispered. "But I didn't have time to tell you. Honestly!

"He only called yesterday night to say he was flying home and coming to the wedding. I didn't want to spoil it for you, but he's only been in town for an hour. I couldn't pass up the chance of his giving me away, could I?"

Her eyes pleaded with her not to be angry, or upset and, of course, Barbara couldn't. Not on Jenny's wedding day . . .

They signed the gold-lettered book. *Jennifer Taylor*, for the last time, she thought, looking at the flamboyant signature, as she signed a neat *Barbara Taylor-Bucy*. She'd kept her first married name and added George's to it, because she didn't feel right being named differently from her daughter.

Adam's father was a short, square man. Walking sedately alongside him in the procession to the church door, she found she missed Jack's tall figure beside her.

How ridiculous, she thought. I'm being a susceptible fool. Five minutes together and already I've succumbed to his charm! Jack and Jenny — father and daughter — charmers both.

The reception was at her brother Al's place. The long, sprinklered lawns and spacious terrace were a perfect setting. Barbara had booked an outside caterer, so once the receiving was over, she had little to do.

Her ex-husband stuck to her side and shared in all the congratulations. White-coated waiters came up with silver trays. She took a glass of champagne.

"Could you bring me a mineral water, please, when you come round again?" Jack asked and the waiter nodded before disappearing into the crowd.

"Most people would think their daughter's wedding an excuse for letting go."

His smile was wry. "I haven't had a drink for five years. And I mean to stay that way." His look was intense, meaningful.

"Why didn't you stop when you were young? For our sake?"

"I couldn't. Keeping you and Jenny should have been the biggest incentive, but I suppose I wasn't ready. No-one else can take a decision like that for you, Barbs."

B ARBS! He was the only person in the world who'd called her that silly name.

She sipped her champagne, lowering her eyes from that too-intense gaze.

"Well, you look great on it, anyway," she told him quietly.

When he spoke again, it was with a trace of awkwardness.

"I'm sorry about your husband."

My husband, she thought crazily, but you're my husband! No, no, George, I don't mean that. Was it the champagne that was doing this to her?

"Are you lonely?" Jack asked abruptly.

She tried to consider the question with honesty.

"Sometimes. There are good things — like having a feminine bedroom to myself, staying in, or going out when I want to, eating in front of the TV."

"I know." He smiled. "I've done all that for years — except for the feminine bedroom."

They laughed. The champagne was relaxing Barbara.

"I haven't always been alone," he said, waiting for her reaction.

"I know. But you don't have to explain to me."

"I'm not explaining. Just putting the record straight. We should start with a clean sheet."

Start! What did he mean? They'd "started" and "finished" a long time ago.

"We've a lot of catching up to do. One day, soon, we'll do it."

"You're assuming a lot." Barbara heard her own snappish voice, but she couldn't help it. Did he believe she'd just been waiting for him to come back?

"Wow!" He blinked. "I've just remembered why I called you Barbs."

Jenny came up to them, her eyes bright.

"Hello, Mum. Has anyone introduced you to my dad?"

Barbara looked at her gorgeous daughter and sighed. "You're so young to be married."

"Exactly the same age as you were when you married me." Jack's arm had gone round Jenny's slim waist and he was looking down into her face.

"And look how that turned out!" Barbara said sharply.

Both pairs of dark eyes turned indignantly back to her.

"Mum!" Jenny was shocked, but Jack answered seriously.

"It turned out wonderfully for ten years. And even then, we still loved each other. You hated me for what I was doing to you both — I hated me, too."

"Poor Daddy." Jenny gave him a resounding kiss on the cheek before moving off again to find her bridegroom.

She turned back and kissed Barbara, too, hissing in her ear, "Be nice to him, Mum."

They were alone again. Or as alone as they could be in the crowd, standing, facing each other.

Barbara tried to make amends. "I divorced a man who was basically kind and good, because he was going through a bad patch."

"So you should have." Jack came to her defence. "I had choices, and so did you."

"Do you remember . . ." They said it together, then stopped.

How did it happen that they were holding hands, Barbara wondered. Jack's warm clasp was achingly familiar.

"Jack, people are looking." She tried to pull her hand away.

"Let them. Know what they're thinking, Barbs? That we've found each other again. And they'd be right. We have, haven't we?"

She didn't answer. She was feeling like a girl on her first date . . . Or like a lost bird, which had found its way home. But birds can be caged . . .

Did she want this? Was she prepared to make the sacrifices that would be needed? Give up all the little bonuses . . .

Jack saw her hesitation. The new, loving confidence on his face changed to uncertainty.

"Barbs?" It was a question.

"Yes, Jack!" She smiled at him. "We've found each other again."

Choices, he'd said. Well, she'd just made one — for better or for worse. □

THAT FIRST BIG STEP

I'M scared, Gran," Alex said. "I know it sounds silly, but I'm scared."

She looked up quickly. *"Does* it sound silly?"

Ellen smiled. "No, love. It doesn't sound silly at all. I think we're all a bit wary of anything new. Leaving home, going to university — well, it's a big step.

"You just have to remember that it's what you've worked for, what you've wanted . . ."

"I know." Alex sighed. "And I'm looking forward to it — really. It's just that — well, none of my friends are going, they're all staying here and getting jobs — and I can't stop thinking how much I'm going to miss you and Dad."

"And we'll miss *you,*" Ellen said gently. "But you'll be fine once you settle in, and we're always here if you need us.

"Think of your Aunt Stephanie. She wasn't much older than you when she left everything she knew — and she went much farther than you'll be going. She was scared, too, but she went because she loved Greg so much."

by ANGELINA SPENCER

"I'm not in love." Alex smiled wryly.

"No, not yet, but you want to study, don't you?" her grandmother reminded her. "You love learning, and you want a good job. If you want something enough, it doesn't matter how scared you are."

Ellen hugged Alex. "You'll be all right, don't you worry. And whatever happens, you've got your old gran."

"You're not old," Alex said lovingly. "But you're right, I know. Once I'm used to it, I'll be fine."

She drifted away and the house fell silent.

ELLEN sat, gazing out of the window, but she saw little of the peaceful and beautiful garden beyond. She was thinking about the past — and Stephanie, her longed-for daughter who'd finally arrived when her brother, David, was almost seventeen.

Right from the start they'd been so close, and after Ellen's husband died, they'd been closer still.

Ellen would never forget how she had felt when her daughter fell in love with Greg and realised she wanted to spend her life with him.

Greg was a kind and lovely man, but he was returning to Australia, and he wanted to take Stephanie with him — and Stephanie wanted to go.

Those had been bittersweet, beautiful, painful days. So happy for her daughter, Ellen had known, too, how much she'd miss her. But she'd smiled and kissed her and wished her well — and a tragic twist of fate had meant she'd barely had time to mourn . . .

The sudden death of David's wife had left him with Alex, his seven-year-old daughter and no idea how he'd cope. When he'd turned to his mother, Ellen hadn't hesitated. Both were lonely, both needed someone, and sad, bewildered Alex needed her grandma. Twelve years later, she was with them still.

She'd never regretted it. They'd saved her, just as she'd saved them. It had been wonderful to see Alex grow up so lovely, so beautiful, and so very like Stephanie, the daughter she still missed so much.

Now Alex was ready to leave her, to move on. And Stephanie . . .

Stephanie had a baby daughter of her own, and she wanted her mother to see her. Ellen wanted to go — but it was so expensive, so far. She'd rarely ever been farther than the next county.

"We can't afford to come over, Mum," Stephanie had said in her letter. "But we can afford to pay for you. Please come, Mum. I'd so love to see you again, and I'd love you to see the baby . . ."

I can't, love, Ellen whispered, as the words still ran through her head. I'd like to, but it's just so far from home . . .

She smiled ruefully. Small wonder she understood Alex's qualms — her own fears were the same. But Alex would be fine. The young usually were.

For her it was different. She was too old for adventure now. For her there would only ever be dreams — and the memories of what might have been.

D AYS whirled by in a frenzy of packing and plans, while Alex veered between excitement and apprehension.

"I wish I could make time stop for a while," she told Ellen. "It's going so fast . . ."

She knew about Stephanie.

"Maybe I should go to Australia and you go to university," she joked. "I could just about cope with that — since I know it won't happen."

The last night came, then the last morning. The three of them were tense and quiet, knowing how much they would miss each other; shrinking away from saying so, afraid to tempt the tears they all knew were lurking.

Soon, they were on their way. Driving steadily, David glanced up at the mirror.

"All right with what we arranged, Alex?" he asked. "Come home for the weekend after the first three weeks, OK? Come earlier if you need to, but stick it out if you can. Give yourself time to settle."

"And ring us any time," Ellen urged. "We're not very far away, remember, only at the other end of the phone."

Then suddenly the car was slowing, and a sign with the name of her hall of residence loomed above a gate.

The next moments were a blur. Students welcomed them and led Alex to her room. David carried cases down unfamiliar corridors. Ellen helped her granddaughter to unpack.

Then soon, too soon, it was time for them to leave.

"Well, love, this is it," Ellen said gently. "We must be off. Now, remember, call us if you need anything at all. Good luck, love."

"Good luck," her father echoed lovingly, and hugged her. "Have a grand time, chick."

"I will, Dad. Thanks," Alex whispered. Her eyes were perilously bright, but she was smiling. "Have a safe journey, now. Take care . . ."

There was a catch in her voice.

"Time to go." Ellen smiled and gave Alex a hug. "Have a lovely time, darling. We'll be seeing you."

A LEX closed the door and gazed silently around the unfamiliar room. Bookshelves waited to be filled. Her clothes hanging in the cupboard looked as though they belonged to someone else. Everything seemed so empty and strange.

Suddenly there was a knock on the door and almost with relief she went to answer it.

"Hello, I think we're neighbours," her visitor began. "I'm in the room next door. I'm Kim —"

Alex returned the friendly smile.

"I'm Alex," she said. "Short for Alexandra. Hi, it's nice to meet you."

Kim drifted into the room, peering through the window.

"Nice view," she commented. "The same as mine. It's a beautiful garden, isn't it? I saw your family leaving, a while ago. Your father and — was that your mother?"

"My gran," Alex explained quietly. "She's brought me up since my mum died when I was seven."

"Oh, I'm sorry," Kim answered softly. She looked at Alex with real compassion in her eyes. "That must have been hard."

"It was," Alex agreed, "but Gran made it easier. I don't know what we'd have done without her."

Again she remembered that now she *was* without her, and again she felt overwhelmed.

Kim was gazing out of the window.

"It's been nice seeing so many people arriving. I've been here for a a week now almost on my own," she explained. "With coming from Hong Kong, you see, I had to come earlier.

"Well, anyway." She smiled brightly. "How'd you like a walk round the hall? I could give you a guided tour. I've found my way around, almost . . ."

The day passed in a blur of new sights and new faces and a tide of new names Alex knew she'd never remember. Then finally, with the hall settling down for the night, she returned to her room. For the first time, she was truly alone.

Alex looked around. It seemed a little more familiar now, though only a little. She did some last-minute tidying, hoisted her suitcase on to the wardrobe, then, getting into bed, lay very still and tried to sleep.

Muffled footsteps passed the door. strange sounds echoed, voices drifted. Distantly, someone laughed. Loneliness welled and mental pictures of home bloomed vividly.

Alex turned restlessly. Lights glowed beyond the windows. The echoing sounds seemed hollow now. She felt herself drifting . . .

SHE was at university, but it was a mistake. She knew she'd never cope. The lectures were beyond her, the place was enormous, she'd never find her way round in a million years. Everyone else seemed so relaxed, so confident, and she knew she'd never belong!

She woke in a panic — and she was in her bed at home. Her grandmother was coming. Alex sat up and reached out to her as the tears poured.

"Oh, Gran, I'm glad it was a dream," she sobbed. "I never want to go away again —"

Her eyes opened. She was lying in the half-darkness of her room in the hall. The dream had been a dream. Homesickness welled as her disappointment struck home, and hearing the crying she'd heard in the dream, she thought she might still be dreaming . . .

No. She was awake — and she *could* hear crying. It seemed to be coming from the room next door.

Alex scrambled out of bed, and pulling on her dressing-gown went to the door. The dimly-lit corridor was empty and hushed. The muffled sobbing grew clearer and sharper.

Part 4

THE triumphant Highlanders were now ready to march into England, and in following the Prince's trail they must make a long journey as far as Derby. In London there was panic when news filtered through that an army of wild Highlanders was bearing down on them.

However, although the Prince was all for advancing farther, his advisers warned him that there were now two large armies ready to swoop upon him — one led by the Duke of Cumberland and the other by General Wade, of road and bridge-building fame.

Against his will, Bonnie Prince Charlie agreed to turn back, and a long retreat was begun, eventually to culminate at Culloden, not far from Inverness. And here came a direct confrontation with the Duke of Cumberland's much larger army of Government troops.

For a second Alex hesitated, then knocked on Kim's door.

The crying stopped. Then, subdued and strained, a voice said, "Who's that?"

"It's me," Alex whispered. "Alex Miller, from next door. Are you all right?"

Footsteps padded across the floor and the door opened. Kim stood in her nightdress, her eyes swollen with tears.

"Come in," she said quietly, and turned away.

Alex followed her into the room and closed the door.

The two girls sat together on the bed.

"I've told myself not to be so silly," Kim said, half-smiling. "I mean, this is just what I wanted. I wanted to come to Britain. I wanted to study here.

"It's just — that it's so far, so different. I miss my family, and I can't go home till summer because it's so expensive.

"I'd have been all right," she went on shakily, "but last night my parents phoned. Oh, Alex — they sounded so near, and they were thousands of miles away . . ."

Tears poured down her face. Alex stared, appalled, and as tears

77

stung her own eyes she reached out to hug Kim.

"I wonder if everyone feels the same," she said when they were calmer. "I mean, in a way it's the same for all of us.

"It's the first time most of us have been away from home. Maybe everyone else feels it too and hides it the way we do."

"Maybe you're right." Kim smiled. "There's certainly no question of giving up — I worked too hard to get here. I suppose we all did, and I couldn't let everyone down. I couldn't let *myself* down . . ."

"That's how I feel," Alex admitted. "You know, my gran said all this to me. I'm not sure I understood then, but I do now.

"She said something else, too. She said I'd be fine once I settled in. When you think about it, it's only natural. There'd be something wrong with your family if you *didn't* mind leaving them.

"But that doesn't mean we won't get used to it and be happy here."

"Maybe we will," Kim whispered, smiling. "Maybe we all will. After all, it can only get easier, can't it?"

"Sure." Alex smiled too. "Sure, it's going to get easier."

AND it did. A whirl of registrations left no time for brooding, and once lectures began it was easier still. Swiftly and surely, university wrapped them into its world. At the end of the week, Alex could phone her family and tell them, honestly, that she loved it.

"Oh, that's good, darling. Didn't I tell you? I said you'd be fine, didn't I?" Ellen reminded her.

"Yes, Gran, you did." Alex laughed. "But you know what helped me most? There's a girl here from Hong Kong, Gran, and she was so homesick. She was just like me, only it was so much harder for her.

"She's OK now, we both are — but it made all the difference, listening to her. It made me see how silly I'd been."

"Not silly, love. It's never silly to mind parting." She could almost hear Ellen's smile. "But I'm glad you're enjoying yourself. Do you want to speak to Dad now?"

Handing the phone to David, leaving the two of them talking, Ellen moved away to the living-room. She re-read Stephanie's letter. Her eyes ran over the lines, though she knew it all by heart.

"Please come, Mum. We'd both love to see you. I can't tell you how much.

"And we want you to see Melissa. She won't be a baby for ever, and we so much want you to see her now."

Everything had changed, and all too soon they would change again. Stephanie was right — her baby wouldn't be a baby for ever.

There was something else, too. She sensed that Stephanie wanted and needed her, just as Alex had, for so long.

What had she said to Alex? "If you want something badly enough, it doesn't matter how scared you are. You reach out, and take it. I'm coming, Stephanie," she silently told her daughter. "I'm coming, my darling, and I'll see you very soon . . ." □

It Takes Two To Tango!

IF her husband, Doug, hadn't arranged to go to the rugby international without consulting her, Sue Stevens probably wouldn't have thought twice about the notice she'd seen in a shop window.

"You wouldn't mind if I go, would you?" he'd said, in the sort of voice that defied discussion. "Freddie's managed to get hold of a couple of tickets."

"No — of course I don't."

She shouldn't have said it, but she did.

by MARGARET WADDINGHAM

There he goes, she thought meanly, off on a jolly jaunt without me. I thought retirement was supposed to be a time when we could do things together? Some hope!

"How would you like to go to a tea dance?" she asked.

He looked at her cautiously over the top of his glasses.

"A what?"

"A tea dance."

"What on earth's that?"

"A dance at teatime, with afternoon tea instead of a bar. You know, dancing, like we used to do?"

"*We* used to do?"

"All right — like I used to. Though we *have* been a few times. Not very often though."

"Because I've got two left feet!"

"Proper dances, like the quickstep and the waltz and the tango. No disco, I promise," Sue wheedled.

"No hip wriggling?"

"Promise. No hip wriggling."

"Oh, well, then —" He returned to his newspaper. "That's no fun!"

"Oh, Doug!" Sue said, exasperated. "We're supposed to be finding things to do together now we've retired. Apart from going to the Garden Club once a month and watching rugby on Saturdays, we see each other less now than we did when we were working."

"I thought that was enough." He looked pained.

"No, it's not enough!" Sue snapped. "Just think of all the things you do without me. You fish, you play bowls, you go bird watching . . ."

"But I've done all that for years, and you always said you didn't mind. You could join me, you know. You could come fishing with me."

"I couldn't. I couldn't bear to handle all those beastly little maggots."

"Bowls, then. You could come bowling."

"It's a men's club," she pointed out patiently.

"Bird watching?"

"At five o'clock in the morning?"

"I don't always go at five o'clock in the morning," he murmured.

"Usually. Anyway, it never seems to be a very sensible time to me."

"It is to the birds!"

Sue realised that for the first time in an age, they were very nearly arguing.

Doug reached over and put his hand on hers.

"Well, at least you like rugby."

"I tolerate it." She snatched her hand away. "I tolerate it, because otherwise we wouldn't even see each other at the weekend in winter!"

"I thought you liked it." His tone was injured. "And we see plenty of each other on top of that!"

"You know what I mean. Don't be irritating!" she retorted.

"Oh, Sue!" Doug groaned and ran his fingers through his thick, grey hair. "Does it have to be dancing? Can't we think of something else?"

"I have thought of something else," Sue persisted. "A tea dance."

"But I've no sense of rhythm. My brain's too far from my feet to send out the right signals," he protested.

"That's because you've never really learned. I'm sure if you did you'd enjoy it. We could have lessons together, you know."

"I'd look a fool."

"Oh . . . " she said, suddenly losing patience. "You're impossible, Doug Stevens!"

She flounced out of the room. It was a long time since she had flounced anywhere, she reflected, assembling silver polish and cloths and lining up cutlery ready for cleaning. Especially, she thought, rubbing viciously at a spoon, especially over such a trivial matter.

The trouble was, it didn't seem to be trivial any more. Every time Doug went fishing or played bowls — or even took out the dog, at a time when she couldn't go, too — she felt more and more resentful.

THE notice beguiled her each time she passed. It was like a beckoning finger that she couldn't resist.

Join the Tea Dance Set. Enjoy dances as you remember them, over a leisurely afternoon tea . . .

In her mind, her feet waltzed down the High Street, quickstepped through the supermarket, tangoed round the bus station.

From time to time, she said, "I suppose you haven't changed your mind about the tea dance, have you?"

But Doug never had.

She found Vera reading the notice one day.

"It sounds nice, don't you think?" she said.

"It sounds wonderful, Sue." Vera sounded wistful. "I only wish I could get Tom to go to something like that."

"Doesn't he dance?"

Vera looked at her.

"Shall we say — he has a unique sense of rhythm!"

"Same with Doug, but I'm sure it's because he's never learned properly. I think he'd enjoy it, if only he'd give it a chance."

"I'd love to do a spot of real dancing again," Vera murmured.

"Oh, so would I . . . quicksteps and waltzes. And the tango — especially the tango. I used to love that."

They turned away from the window and began to walk down the road.

"How's retirement?" Vera asked.

"Wonderful," Sue said defensively.

Vera looked at her closely.

"You sure? That didn't sound very convincing."

"Oh, it's wonderful, all right. Apart from one thing."

F

Sue took a deep breath. Well, why not tell Vera?

"I was looking forward to this being a time when we could share lots of interests. Doug's always had so many, and I always thought that we could hit on one or two things that we'd like to do together."

"And haven't you?"

"Not exactly. That's why I was so interested in the dancing idea, but I haven't managed to persuade him. I'll just have to think of something else.

"There are some women —" she went on, neatly sidestepping a young mother with a pushchair " — who find retirement all too much. They say they can't stand having their husbands around all day."

"Hah," Vera said. "I wonder what that's like. I hardly ever seem to see Tom."

They went on down the busy street in silence for a while.

"Of course, it has been known for women to go to these dances with a friend." Sue's voice was thoughtful.

"It has, hasn't it?" Vera glanced sidelong at her. "Are you thinking what I'm thinking?"

Sue looked up at the sky and sucked in her cheeks. Then she smiled.

"Yes, I rather think I am."

IT all fitted in very well. When she got home, Doug asked, rather sheepishly, whether she would mind if he went to an away match next Thursday. Bowling, of course.

"As long as you don't object to me doing something that day, too," Sue remarked.

"Of course not." He looked at her in surprise. "I'd be glad if you did, then I wouldn't feel guilty. What is it?"

"I'd like to go to this tea dance I've been telling you about. I've met someone else who'd very much like to go."

"What someone else?" He looked mildly alarmed.

"Vera Thomson. Remember? She used to come to the WI."

"Two *women*?" He was aghast. "Two women on their own at a dance?"

"Why not?"

"You're married!"

"So is Vera." She laughed. "Would you prefer if I found another man to take me?"

He ignored that.

"And you're over sixty!"

"Don't be pompous," she snapped.

"Sue, darling. I'm not being pompous. But you do have to think about these things."

"What things?" she demanded indignantly. "I'm still mobile, aren't I? If the undertaker's waiting for me to keel over, he'd better get a very long book to read.

"Just occasionally, Doug —" she added, prodding his chest "— just

82

Adventurous Spirit

IN the mountains of Wales, on the
hillsides and dales,
We wandered and plotted our
course;
We travelled to places, where nomadic
races
Lived lives which the experts
endorsed.

Down rivers we went, deep in caves
with heads bent,
In forests we fought off the flies;
Horse trekking we tried, donkey, bike,
camel ride,
Hang-gliding, we flew through the
skies.

Now whatever we claim, take a map
and then aim
To imagine it all — and don't pay!
For it's not what it seems, we've been
there in our dreams,
In the brochures we picked up
today!
— *Chrissy Greenslade.*

occasionally, I might like to spend some time doing something I really love. Like dancing!"

★　　　★　　　★　　　★

It was a huge success. Sitting at one of the small tables round the dance floor at the Court Hotel. Vera and Sue drank tea from pink-and-white tea cups, ate scones, compared notes over the way their husbands had taken the news, and laughed.

"They sound as bad as each other!" Vera chuckled. "What on earth makes them think age has anything to do with dancing?"

Sue was listening to the music.

"A tango," she said happily. "Shall we see if we can find out?"

She was full of the good time she'd had when she got home and Doug listened politely.

"Won't you think about coming?" she finished coaxingly. "It's all very — gentle stuff. Nothing that could possibly make you embarrassed." She put her hands on his chest and smoothed his shirt collar.

"Several people don't really know what they're doing, but everyone's so friendly it doesn't matter. And Fred and Ginger . . . "

"Fred and Ginger?" he echoed incredulously.

"The organisers. That's what they call themselves."

Doug shook his head and sat down at the kitchen table.

"Well, anyway, Fred and Ginger are so good. If they see anyone who looks a bit lost, they go and help them out. It's such fun, Doug. I wish you'd come," she wheedled.

"But if you're enjoying yourself with Vera, what's the point in my spoiling it?"

She looked at him.

"You're changing your tune, aren't you? Last week, you didn't even want me to go with Vera." She perched in front of him on the edge of the table.

"You wouldn't spoil it, Doug. It's good fun with Vera, but I'd much rather be dancing with you than anyone else. Especially another woman!"

"What about Fred? Couldn't he dance with you?"

"He does," she said, slightly exasperated. "But I want you."

"I don't like dancing."

"I don't like rugby!"

"I'd feel a fool."

"I married one!" Sue began to chop parsley for a sauce with more energy than usual.

SHE and Vera went dancing again the following week and once more she came home full of enthusiasm.

"It's wonderful," she said. "A lovely floor and a very good band — just four of them, who don't play so loudly that you can't hear yourself think.

"And do you know? I can still tango! I love the tango. And everyone's so nice. It really doesn't matter if you can't dance, Doug . . ."

"I expect you'll be going off with Vera again, then?"

"No, Vera's got to go to Wales to look after her daughter for a few weeks. And I certainly don't want to go on my own."

"Well, I'm afraid I can't go." He avoided her eyes. "I've just joined up for a fortnight of DIY classes."

She stared at him in amazement. "You? DIY?"

"Yes, a fortnight of daily classes works out cheaper than a whole term of evening classes.

"You know how hopeless I am at DIY. I thought now that I've got the time . . . besides, think of the money we'll save."

"Ha! And how much of the money you save are we going to have to spend to put things right after you've been at them with your DIY, Doug Stevens?"

Hurt, he chose not to answer that.

How mean of me, Sue thought, and wished she hadn't said it.

Just for one moment, she did contemplate going to the tea dance on her own the following Thursday.

Only for one moment. She wasn't the sort to go to places on her own. She got out her sewing machine and finished off the dress she'd been making instead.

It was her birthday the following Thursday. At breakfast time, Doug kissed her and gave her a card.

"I've got to go out this morning, darling. It's the last of my classes. You don't mind, do you?"

"No," she said automatically, trying hard not to.

"One other thing. You can't have your present until later, I'm afraid."

Oh, heavens, she thought, it's something he's made for me at his class! She tried hard to smile cheerfully at the prospect.

"Freddie and Mary want us to go over this afternoon for a birthday tea," he added.

This time her smile was of genuine pleasure.

"How lovely. I haven't seen Mary for ages."

"I've arranged a taxi to collect you at about half-past two."

"A taxi?" She was puzzled.

"Well, I'll need the car. My class finishes a bit too late to get back, have lunch and get out again in time," he explained.

"I suppose that makes sense," Sue muttered as he headed for the door.

THE taxi was on time. The only problem was that it didn't take her to Freddie and Mary's house.

"No," she said to the driver as he pulled up somewhere in town. "This isn't where you're supposed to take me!"

"These were my instructions, love," the taxi driver said. "Very clear and all paid up. Are you going to get out? It's a nice hotel, isn't it?"

"Oh, yes," she said, dazed. "I know it quite well."

Sue got out, and stared up at the Court Hotel. A uniformed commissionaire appeared at her side.

"Mrs Stevens?"

"Yes, that's me." She was startled.

"Would you like to follow me, madam?"

Up the white steps, through the rotating doors, and along wide, blue-carpeted passages to the room where the tea dance was held . . . She grew more intrigued by the moment.

The commissionaire held open the door for her and led her to a small table.

"Doug!" she said in astonishment.

Doug, in his best grey suit, his face wreathed in the broadest of smiles, got to his feet.

"Happy birthday, darling." He kissed her gently.

"I don't believe this! Just a moment while I pinch myself."

"Don't waste time doing that," he retorted. "They're just starting a tango, and Ginger has spent a long time teaching me how to do it!"

He took her hands in his, and led her on to the dance floor.

"This is your birthday present," he said, his face close to hers.

She moulded her body to his, and their feet followed the music. Doug was light on his feet, and so confident!

"DIY lessons?" she said happily. "May you be forgiven!"

"I think I will." He grinned. "After all, it was a very good cause."

And he swung her round with such expertise that Fred and Ginger smiled with approval. □

"N O! I just won't allow it!" Jill declared. Her son, Greg, had just reminded her of her promise, on the evening of his fourteenth birthday.

She'd forgotten all about it — but Greg hadn't. No wonder he'd grinned with such satisfaction as he'd blown out his candles.

"But you promised!" Greg insisted.

"You said I could go with Dad when I got to be fourteen. Now I'm fourteen and I'm going with Dad next Saturday. You can't go back on your word!"

"I didn't realise you'd be fourteen so soon," Jill protested, looking at her husband, Stephen for support.

But Stephen kept his mouth shut. He just sat there eating his share of birthday cake.

"I'm sorry, Greg, but I'd worry myself sick about you doing what your dad does — at your age. I shouldn't have made that promise at the time.

"I didn't realise you'd take it so seriously, or that four years would rush by so fast!" Jill felt she was being reasonable. "I mean, really, you're still too young for something as dangerous as that!

"Stephen, don't you agree?"

"I didn't make any promises," Stephen muttered, wearing that all-too-familiar, "I'm staying out of this," look.

Greg looked miserable as he indignantly poked at the crumbs on his plate.

Now I've ruined his birthday, Jill thought to herself, and all because I love him so much!

Of course she wanted to

ONLY ONE WAY TO LEARN

blame Stephen. Wasn't it his fault?

Jill found herself thinking back to the time when they'd first met. He'd warned her, but she hadn't really thought much about it then.

Stephen looked normal enough. He was tall and lean, with sandy, brown hair and hazel eyes. Not handsome, but rather attractive in a rough-and-ready way. In the beginning, just a shy, awkward furniture salesman who helped Jill choose a new breakfast-table.

She remembered how he'd blushed and mumbled, "Don't suppose you'd care to join me for lunch?" after handing her the sales receipt and how, much to his surprise, she'd accepted the offer.

"I've got something to tell you," he'd announced, after the third or fourth date. Taking a deep breath, he went on. "I'm a pot-holer."

Apparently Stephen's idea of fun was spending at least one weekend a month grovelling down damp, dark passages hundreds of feet underground.

Jill imagined what it must be like and decided it would be horrible — a claustrophobic nightmare! Nevertheless something about it intrigued her. At

by
LISA
AMMERMAN

nineteen, she liked to think of herself as a sort of dare-devil too. She loved sail-boarding, hiking, and riding on the pillion of a motor-bike — so why should pot-holing be any different?

"You don't mind?" Stephen asked again.

"Of course not," she said.

THEY married not long after that, and for many years Jill didn't mind him spending his Saturdays in underground caves.

"To each his own," was her favourite expression.

Anyway, Stephen wasn't the type who insisted his wife share his hobbies. Jill might understand his need to explore, but she certainly couldn't see any reason why she should go where no human being was ever meant to be! So Stephen's hobby hadn't caused any friction between them — until now, that is.

Sitting together at the dining-room table, with a fast-growing, younger version of Stephen, Jill realised that things had changed. At some point during the past fifteen years, her dare-devil tolerance level had begun to weaken. Now it had snapped and all because her son wanted to follow his father's footsteps.

The silence was becoming unbearable. Jill cleared her throat. Maybe she could try stalling for more time, and in a flash of inspiration she recalled some technical detail Stephen had told her about.

"Look, Greg," she pleaded. "I'll let you go, but not before you've completed the Single Rope Technique Course. Then you'll be properly qualified to go caving, like your dad."

"But that could take months!" Greg exclaimed. "And besides, lots of caves don't even need SRT. Isn't that right, Dad?"

Stephen nodded before taking another sip of coffee.

"So couldn't you bring me down one of the easy caves first, with no SRT involved?"

"I could," Stephen replied. "But I won't unless your mother approves."

Greg turned to his mum.

"No!" she repeated. "Go ahead and hate me, but it's far too dangerous. I can't let you take the risk."

"Dad's been doing it for yonks, and he hasn't had a single accident," Greg insisted.

"Not that he'd ever tell me if he did," Jill added. "It's enough worrying about one, let alone two. I won't have it."

"Most bad accidents happen right at home," Stephen stated, suddenly discarding his impartiality. "Don't talk about what's dangerous unless you know what you're talking about."

"Oh, so I don't know what I'm talking about then?"

"Nope! How can you? You've never been down a cave. If you had, you'd realise how safe it really is when you're careful and do it properly."

"OK then!" Jill suddenly had a thought. At least this was a way of postponing the inevitable. "How about if I go down a cave first, and see for myself just how safe it really is?"

She paused, savouring her brilliant solution to the problem. Not only was she being fair and reasonable, she was also showing how prepared she was to justify her argument.

Stephen almost choked on his coffee.

"Did I hear right? Did you just say you'll go down a cave? You're not serious?"

"I am serious! I'll go and see for myself," Jill said. "But you have to agree, both of you, that if I come out of it — alive — and remain convinced about the dangers, Greg waits until he's older."

"It's a deal!" shouted father and son, simultaneously. The two of them looked at Jill quite amazed, as if Mum, the Worrier, had suddenly turned into Mum, the Warrior.

A WEEK later, plodding up a Derbyshire hillside toward Winchell's Cave, Jill could only regret her impetuous decision. What on earth was she doing?

She wasn't as fit as Stephen and it seemed an unbearably long journey across the fields toward the cave as Stephen and two other members of his caving club marched eagerly ahead.

The early morning September air was clear and crisp. Derbyshire was as lovely as ever, with lush, green, rolling hills criss-crossed with drystone walls and dotted with sheep. But Jill couldn't enjoy the surroundings. She was too busy trying to stifle a mounting wave of hysteria.

"Not far to go," Stephen promised, stopping to let her catch up. "It's just over this hill. You can hear the stream, can't you?"

"Yes, I hear it," Jill answered, pausing to adjust her grip on helmet and dangling battery pack.

"You all right?"

"Fine!" No doubt about it, under the bright smile she was absolutely petrified, as they drew nearer to the entrance of the cave.

"It's not as bad as it looks." Stephen smiled sympathetically. "Here, take a closer look, and you can see how it opens up, once you've squeezed through."

Jill took a closer look at the small space in the rock. The hole did indeed appear to grow bigger and wider after the first few feet. But what could she really see in the darkness?

Stephen switched on her helmet lantern.

"I'll go first, and you can follow right behind me."

Before Jill could protest, he'd already wedged himself through the hole. The next minute nothing but his hand remained, groping blindly in the sunlight.

"Come on, Jill. You can do it!"

His voice held a ring of confidence. Jill took a deep breath, grabbed Stephen's hand, and squirmed through the hole.

After a few feet of unexpected and blissful space, the passage narrowed again.

"Wait a minute," she whispered anxiously to Stephen after they'd made their way along a narrow passage for what seemed like ages.

"How long is it going to be like this?"

"Not long," Stephen replied.

"You're fine, you're doing great," he insisted as they squeezed through a narrow gap in the rock.

Jill felt so claustrophobic she wanted to scream. How could Stephen be so nonchalant about them crawling through spaces only centimetres wider than they were, themselves?

Stephen coaxed her on, letting her think he'd not noticed her anxiety. He continued chatting and joking in a constant effort to take her mind off her state of panic. They continued like this for several minutes, then strangely enough, as soon as she reasoned with herself that JILL was the only person who would be able to get JILL out of there — she relaxed. She calmed down.

Stranger still, she began actually to enjoy the experience and then she remembered a quote she once heard. "The only thing to fear is fear itself."

So that was it! An important lesson, she realised, and something she'd want her son to learn as well.

A FEW yards ahead and the passage opened up into an enormous cavern.

The noise was deafening! Waterfalls crashed and cascaded from the dark, gloomy hollows above, into swirling pools of translucent bubbles, bouncing against smooth, sculptured rock.

"It's beautiful!" Jill exclaimed, astonished by the unexpected brilliance and clarity of the light.

"It's over a hundred feet high!" Ian, one of their companions, remarked, shining his lantern along the cavern walls.

"And just look how the rocks sparkle in the light."

After describing a bit about the rock formations and the minerals that shone diamond-bright in the glow of their lanterns, the three men proudly clambered toward a corner of the chamber.

The sound of human voices echoed merrily round the cave.

"Jill! Come and look at this! And this!"

"You're right! It's worth the effort!" Jill admitted to Stephen.

By the time they'd reached the fourth chamber, she also had to admit she felt quite exhilarated by a renewed sense of daring and self-confidence. At the same time she realised caving needn't be dangerous.

As the day wore on Jill's enthusiasm began to wane. She wanted to stop and rest but Stephen insisted they all keep moving, to keep warm.

When they entered a long passage with just two feet of headroom, Stephen looked worried. The stream had risen more than he'd expected.

Jill's strength was giving out but she assured Stephen the cramped air-space didn't bother her, not any more. She'd come this far. She certainly wasn't going to drop out *now.*

Despite the protective gloves and leg pads, the palms of her hands

Part 5

THE Battle Of Culloden was fought on April 16, 1746. It began at one o'clock and in half an hour the Jacobite army was routed, and the Prince forced to flee to the Western Highlands.

With a band of six horsemen, riding that day and through the night, he reached Fort Augustus and Invergarry Castle, arriving in the early hours. Next day, with three followers, he took the old bridle track along Loch Lochy, then made for Loch Arkaig by way of the wooded Dark Mile. The following day he was on the road again, but now on foot as the Braes of Morar were too rough for horses. As hillwalkers know, this is a boggy, squelchy track to this day!

On the night of the 20th he walked to Borrodale on the shore of the Loch Of The Caves, where he had first landed on the mainland, and then, taking what boat he could, he set sail for Benbecula in the Outer Hebrides.

Following Bonnie Prince Charlie's trail now becomes more and more difficult, for there followed many weeks of privation and hairbreadth escapes from capture.

Eventually, on South Uist, he met Flora Macdonald, and had it not been for this brave young lady he would certainly have been caught, for he was now hemmed in by Government troops and ever-vigilant ships.

---

and her knees ached not only from the cold, but from the constant bumping and sliding over the sharp pebbles under the stream.

Now she wanted to overcome her fears, for her own sake.

Maybe she'd rather not be here, crawling on her hands and knees with the stream running just below her chin — but she was facing a challenge, wasn't she? She was pushing herself hard, and it felt good!

"Not much longer," Stephen promised.

Sure enough, after a few minutes Jill pulled herself up again on two feet. She'd used up her last bit of nerve and strength, but the low-roofed passage had led into a spacious chamber like a cathedral, with a burst of sunlight breaking through!

Jill's heart sank as soon as she realised Stephen looked concerned. They'd made it all right, only to face a forty-foot climb up a steel ladder to reach the opening. This ladder was secured along-side a waterfall.

"It's usually just a trickle," Stephen explained. "It must be raining outside — despite the good forecast!"

The rain had turned this "trickle" into a gushing torrent, smashing down over the ladder.

Rubbing his chin anxiously, Stephen consulted with Robert and Ian. How were they going to get up?

Ian attempted the ladder first, but the waterfall crashed down on his head and shoulders, making his progress very strenuous and slow.

When he reached the top, he smiled triumphantly but when he

looked at Jill he shook his head and shouted over the deafening din
of the cascade.

"Do you think you'll manage it, Jill? It's a tough climb, and I know
you're tired."

"I can do it," she replied, feeling her pulse quicken at the thought
of attempting the climb. "Yes, I want to do it!"

Spluttering and pulling with all her might against the heavy
bombardment of water, Jill grabbed the rungs of the ladder and
climbed.

M UM, you didn't really climb to the top of that ladder, did you?
Not when the men could have pulled you up?" Greg leaned
forward, hanging on her every word.

For Jill, already back home, was relating the entire story to Greg
over supper.

"It's true, you know, that if you've got the willpower, you can
accomplish almost anything," Jill went on. "And I was absolutely
determined to do it, even though my legs felt like jelly and my arms
felt as if they were being wrenched from my body."

She paused, while Greg waited with baited breath, his jaw hanging
wide open. Meanwhile Stephen looked as if he was having a hard
time trying to hide a smile.

"I concentrated on one thing. Just raising each foot, slowly and
surely. One, then two, then three rungs of the ladder. Slowly but
surely, all the way up to twenty-three."

Jill smiled and shrugged. She decided she'd said enough already.
How could she explain such a personal feeling? In her own mind, she
knew she'd used a hidden reserve of strength she didn't even realise
she had.

"All we could do was watch," Stephen added. "We were so amazed
when she got to the top, that we gave her a big round of applause."

Greg's mouth closed. He looked relieved, but the suspense wasn't
over yet.

"But even so," Stephen went on, "we didn't think you were
strong enough."

"But I knew I was!" Jill replied.

"Well, you convinced us all right." Stephen chuckled. "Why do I
have the feeling you might get hooked on pot-holing, like the rest of
us?"

He winked at Greg. Greg looked at Jill. Jill thought a minute.

"I can't imagine what makes you think that. Because I *never*, ever
want to do that again — ever!"

Father and son watched in stunned silence and dismay as Jill pushed
out her chair from the kitchen table. She stood up with a formidable
look on her face but after moving to the sink, and turning on the taps
for the washing up, she turned to look at them.

Then, much to their surprise, her sud-streaked arm reached out
toward her son, to bestow an unexpected hug.

"So, when are you going, Greg?" □

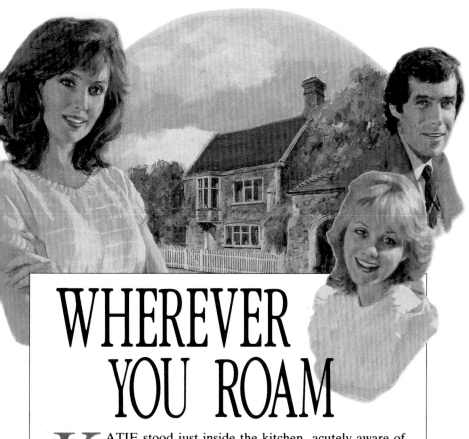

WHEREVER YOU ROAM

KATIE stood just inside the kitchen, acutely aware of her own strangeness and lack of belonging in these surroundings. It was ridiculous! Doreen and she were kith and kin.

A few hours earlier she had scanned the anxious faces lined up in the arrivals lounge of the airport before being met by her sister, Doreen.

After what seemed a lifetime in America, she hadn't recognised her straight away. Maybe it was the different hairstyle . . . It was only when she heard the familiar laugh that she associated the mature woman ahead of her with the cheerful sister she hadn't seen for years.

Then it all came rushing back . . . all they'd shared. Everything they'd done together.

People used to mistake them for twins in their growing years. That was Mum's fault, Katie reflected. Having two daughters so near in age, she used to dress them alike.

by MARY MARSHALL

When they were older, even their boyfriends could hardly tell them apart! A memory of happy days with Johnny and Mark flashed through Katie's mind.

Doreen married Johnny in the end. He was her one and only. Katie couldn't settle for that. She wanted something different. Well — she bit her lip. She certainly got that!

Here, in this modernised kitchen of the home where she'd been brought up, she felt again a distance — a gap that couldn't be bridged.

"Is there anything I can do?" Katie ventured as Doreen bustled around laying out cups and saucers.

"Maybe you'd like to set Mum's tray — there it is in the corner." Doreen nodded in the direction of a kitchen cupboard.

Her fingers traced a faded rose pattern. It was so well-worn and out of place with the rest of the kitchen.

"D'you mean this tray?" she queried.

"That's the one," Doreen agreed, fetching a traycloth from the drawer.

Surely Mum deserved better, Katie thought. What could Doreen be thinking of? Once she was settled, she must have a word with Doreen about it. Meantime, she obediently set out the cup and saucer and buttered a scone.

"Mum will just be waking up," Doreen told her as she handed Katie the laden tray. "Seeing you will give her a lovely surprise. She'd no idea of the time you'd be arriving."

Katie's heart beat fast as she climbed the stairs. How would Mum react to seeing her after all those years? How was she going to explain away not coming home before now? With people criss-crossing the Atlantic every day, any excuse would sound lame.

With luck, she might not have to explain. After all, the family hadn't been too keen on Jamie when she'd introduced him to them. She remembered the disapproval on Dad's face, and how he'd registered it with the slow shake of his head.

"He's not for you, lass," he'd said, when they were alone.

At the time, Katie had thought her dad prejudiced in favour of Mark, who had been her constant companion since leaving school. But Mark had always been there. There was nothing new to find out about him, not like Jamie, who had come from America and could hold Katie spellbound with his accounts of life in the States.

In the end, she'd chosen Jamie.

Everything had seemed wonderful after the wedding. Jamie enjoyed his work as a computer engineer, and Katie was able to carry on working at the factory office.

She saw plenty of the family, though she felt Jamie had never been entirely accepted, and he still hankered to return to the States.

His opportunity came when the company he worked for opened up a branch in New York.

Katie's heart beat fast as she climbed the stairs. How would Mum about. Even Mum and Dad found themselves offering fewer objections. So off they'd gone, the good wishes of the family ringing in their ears.

NOW, she quelled her guilty feelings as she crossed the landing and knocked gently on the bedroom door. There was no sound, so she entered quietly, laying the tray on one side while she opened the curtains.

Her mother stirred. She gave a start when she saw Katie. Then, as recognition dawned, she held out her arms.

Katie wrapped her own strong arms around her mother, her hair brushing against the fine skin, and tears falling unashamedly.

"Oh Mum, it's been so long."

"Too long," the older woman agreed. "Now, let me have a proper look at you."

She pulled herself up on her pillows, and Katie sat back on her heels clutching her knees whilst her mum gazed intently into her face.

"Mm," she said at last, "you could put on a bit of weight. You're far too thin."

Katie laughed, jumping to her feet.

"It's healthy to be thin, nowadays," she protested. "Anyway, I've brought your cup of tea, so let me see you drink it before it's too cold."

Sitting by her, Katie watched her mum drink from the cup.

"That's better," Mum said, draining the last drop. She patted the side of the bed. "Come nearer, and give me all your news."

"I've been busy, Mum. You know I was promoted and it takes a little time to get everything running smoothly and . . ."

"Katie," Mum interrupted, "you don't have to tell me, we understand. It's Jamie, isn't it?" She touched Katie gently.

The bowed head said it all.

"He found someone else, Mum." Her voice was scarcely audible.

"I thought there was more behind your coming home than you told us before," Mum said wisely.

Katie lifted her head to protest, and then realised it was probably true.

Her sudden home-sickness had been caused by a desire to feel loved and cherished once again.

But just now she felt she might have been wrong. The years could leave a gap that might never be filled, and the old guilt feelings returned once more.

"Mum, about Dad . . ." she tried to say, but her mother's hand covered hers.

. . . "Your dad understood, Katie. He always understood."

THE corner of the traycloth accidentally caught on the metal edge of a photograph frame on the bedside cabinet, tumbling it to the floor.

Katie bent to pick it up, and the face of a schoolboy and schoolgirl smiled back at her. He had his arm around her waist.

Katie held the picture frame in her hand for a moment, remembering the photo being taken on that last day of school. They'd all been so excited, looking towards the future!

"An odd choice of photograph, Mum!" Katie observed, laying it carefully back on the cabinet. "You must have a more up-to-date photo of me around the house."

Mum pulled the sheet closer under her chin.

"I always liked that one . . . those were happy times," she commented. "Anyway, you haven't been sending so many photos lately."

Katie sighed, "Now, Mum, I sent you plenty from America."

Her mum looked at Katie, leaving unsaid what they both knew — that Jamie was also in most of the photos she sent.

"I had a feeling you'd be coming on your own this time, and . . ."

"But that's so old and out of date, Mum. It's not really suitable," Katie said reproachfully. "I'll rummage amongst my baggage and try to find something better for you to put on display."

"You'll never find a better photograph!" her mum parried as Katie opened the door. "Anyway, Mark likes to see it, too, when he comes to visit me."

Katie stopped abruptly by the door.

"Mark visits you?" she asked incredulously.

Mum nodded.

"If you remember, your dad was very fond of him, and he's been very good to me since Dad died."

"Hasn't he married and settled down with family of his own?"

Mum shook her head.

"He always said he could never find the right girl . . . We'd all thought he'd found the right girl — and then lost her."

There was no answer to that.

Katie let her mother's bedroom door swing shut behind her and went downstairs, her mind in confusion.

She tackled Doreen as she entered the kitchen.

"Doreen, Mum says Mark still visits! I thought he'd be miles away from here by now."

Doreen was carefully basting the meat in the oven and her flushed face appeared over the door.

"Nope," she answered. "He settled in this corner of the world. He always was a homebird, Mark, and you know he got on really well with Dad . . . Apart from being Johnny's best mate."

Katie nodded, putting down the tray.

"Funny he never married."

"Wasn't the marrying kind, if you ask me." Doreen closed the oven door. "Mind you, he always had a yen for you, didn't he?" she suggested mischievously. "Anyway, you'll be able to ask him all the questions you like this evening."

"He's coming this evening?"

Doreen nodded.

"He always comes home with Johnny on a Friday —" She stopped and gazed anxiously at Katie.

"Oh, I'm sorry, Katie, I never thought . . . I hope you don't mind . . . He's done it since Dad died. It's grown into a sort of habit."

Katie shrugged.

She remembered life always had a pattern and predictability here. Dad saw to that.

That's why Jamie had seemed so exciting — had been so unpredictable!

She rinsed the cup and saucer and folded the traycloth. The faded roses were once more exposed — even they seemed to hold a secret she wasn't to share.

"Come and put your feet up for a while," Doreen suggested and Katie followed her sister into the living-room.

She must have dozed off, for when she awoke, Doreen had disappeared back into the kitchen and Johnny and Mark were chattering over her head.

SO you've broken up?" Johnny joked, as he leant down and gave her a brotherly kiss. "You remember Mark, don't you?"

Katie felt at a distinct disadvantage, and started to rise from the chair. Mark held out his hand.

"You don't have to rise for me, Katie — just you sit back and rest. You must be tired after the journey."

He leant down and took her hand and gazed deeply into her face, and she felt decidedly embarrassed. He didn't resemble the boy in the photograph upstairs, any more than she was the girl.

"I must say, you're a sight for sore eyes," he commented.

"I'll go and give Doreen a hand in the kitchen," Johnny said lamely.

There was an awkward silence after he'd left. Where would she begin talking to someone whom she hadn't seen for years, and who'd never been away from home — whilst she had been around the world and back?

She glanced despairingly at the suddenly shy Mark and in desperation she found herself saying, "Mark, have you any idea why Mum insists on having her tea brought on an old tin tray?"

He looked up and suddenly there was the familiar glint of the old Mark shining in his eye, all awkwardness gone.

"Don't you remember, Katie? How could you forget? You bought that tray from your first pay packet. Your mum always felt as long as she held on to that tray, you'd come home — no matter how far you travelled."

The grave, grey eyes were looking questioningly at her. "You have come home, haven't you, Katie?"

He took her hand and suddenly the gap that couldn't be bridged all day seemed to disappear.

Katie took a long deep breath.

"I hope so. I certainly hope so," she whispered. □

Emily's Great

by **MARY CARTER**

A SUDDEN cry of pain startled me and I ran to the open door to see what had happened.

A little blonde girl was lying face down on the Tarmac play area.

I hurried outside, gently picki her up, comforting her.

"Big girls can cry, can't the Meg?" she asked tearfully.

Plan

I was touched by her question.
She was only four years old!

"Of course they can, darling," I replied as we went into the nursery together. "We'll soon have your poor knee clean and feeling much better."

I'd discovered where the first-aid box was on my first day at the nursery, last week, and, having young grandchildren of my own, was able to administer the magic blend of medical and motherly treatment.

Within a few minutes she was showing off the big plaster on her knee.

Then she sat down beside me to have a drink of milk.

"You're a new lady," she announced. "My name's Emily. I've been at the nursery for a long, long, long time, but you only came last week.

"You look like my granny. She had curly hair."

I took this as a compliment and was about to thank her when she spoke again.

"My curly granny died last year. Mummy cried when Grandad telephoned to tell us. That's when my Daddy told me that big girls can cry. I cried — and Daddy did too."

"That was very sad for all of you," I said gently. "You must miss your granny a lot."

"Yes I do, but it'll be lovely when my grandad comes to stay with us again. He takes me out and sometimes he takes me upstairs on a double-decker bus!"

Her eyes widened at the thought of this adventure.

She turned when one of her young friends called her over to the Wendy House.

"I must get back to my house," she said seriously. "I love you, Meg."

The little girl's solemn words brought a lump to my throat, thoughts of my own grandchildren filling my mind.

When my dear husband, Harold, died, I sold my house in the south of England and moved into the flat attached to the home of my son, Paul, and his wife, Jane.

I had always got on well with them and I loved the company of my four grandchildren.

Just as I was beginning to feel really settled, Paul's company had been taken over by a large American firm. They offered him an executive post, with a very good salary — in California.

Jane had urged me to go with them.

"No," I'd said. "You'll have enough to do, sorting out your own lives in a new country. Besides, I would much rather stay here," I'd lied, "I've begun to find my feet."

So the house and granny flat was sold and I bought a new, small garden flat.

As the weeks went by, I found that I missed my young family dreadfully, and the busy, happy routine that we had enjoyed.

I suppose that I missed being useful and needed. The flat took only about an hour a day to clean and tidy and I hadn't really had a chance to make friends nearby.

Then I saw the advert in the local newspaper shop window. A volunteer was needed at the nearby nursery — someone to provide drinks, mop up spills, see to grazed knees and tell stories to the children! They needed a granny!

I went along for a chat and was pleased when I was accepted.

The staff were friendly and appreciative of my help and the children delightful. The building itself was a cheery place to work, with brightly-coloured toys and equipment, the walls covered with the children's own paintings.

Their voices, as they played and talked together, were a tonic. Even before my first morning had ended, I knew that I had made the right decision.

AFTER her fall, Emily adopted me as her special friend and she chattered to me every day.

I had met Emily's mother, Sally, the day after Emily's little accident and she was very friendly.

As my flat was in the road just beyond Sally's house, we started walking home together. I enjoyed chatting to Sally as we walked with Emily holding my hand and Sally pushing the pram which held the baby, Tom.

I discovered that it was soon Emily's birthday.

"You can come to my party," she announced to me at nursery.

"Well you must ask your mummy first," I told her gently.

Sally was smiling when she came to collect Emily the next day.

"Emily says you're invited to her party next Tuesday, Meg. I do hope you can come. When Emily has a plan, there's no peace until it's carried out."

The party was a great success and I must have enjoyed myself as much as the eight young guests.

I was pleased to be able to help Sally and her husband, Richard, entertain the children and stayed behind afterwards to help tidy up.

While Sally and her husband cleared up the awful mess that a successful children's party always leaves behind, Emily and I bathed baby Tom and put him in his cot. Then I bathed Emily, told her a story, and tucked her up in bed.

With the children settled, Richard poured a glass of sherry for everyone.

"That was a great party." Sally sighed, kicking off her shoes wearily. "Our best yet — thanks to you, Meg, with all those super games."

"You've no idea how much *I* enjoyed myself. I should be thanking you for letting me come."

Sally laughed.

"That gives me the perfect opening for the favour we want to ask. Emily says that she wants you to be our baby-sitter. We'd be so happy if you would, and, after today, it's obvious that both the children really love you."

"Well, if Emily says, there's really no more discussion needed," I replied. "I think I'll have to appoint her as my business manager!"

Now there was no time to sit around feeling sorry for myself.

I joined a theatre group, a badminton club, and on Sundays I went out with a rambling club.

With these activities, and my morning work at the nursery, my circle of friends was widening, and I was so much happier.

Once a week we baked at the nursery. The youngsters, in their colourful pinafores, loved to weigh, measure and stir the mixtures.

Just before Easter we made nests out of cornflakes and chocolate. Inside each nest we placed eggs made of peppermint creams.

"Meg, please can I make three nests? One for Mummy, one for Daddy, and one for Grandad. He's coming to stay with us," Emily revealed.

On the last day of term, Sally came to meet Emily with her father. He was a tall, pleasant-looking man with silver hair.

He lifted Emily shoulder-high.

"Well, Mischief, what have you been up to?"

"I've been making something really nice for you with Meg, but it's a secret, isn't it, Meg? I'm not to tell you what it is and you can't have it until Sunday and it's a surprise, isn't it, Meg?"

Breathless after this long statement, she looked at me conspiratorially and smiled.

"And this is Meg."

"Well, you've certainly won this young lady's affection." He smiled easily and I couldn't help smiling back. It was easy to see where Emily got her charm, I thought.

He put Emily down when she struggled and she ran off to collect her paintings, Easter card and the nests.

"Well, Emily said you were staying, Mr . . . ?"

"Grandad's name is Bill," Emily said, returning with her little bag.

"Oh, well, good to meet you, Bill." I smiled.

"And very nice to meet you, Meg," was his laughing reply as they left the hall hand-in-hand.

WHEN the phone rang early on Monday morning I was surprised to hear Sally's voice.

"Meg, could you possibly baby-sit for us this evening, please? Dad and Richard and I have been invited out to dinner with friends. I know it's very short notice, but we would love to go."

"That's no problem, Sally. What time shall I come?"

"Could you make it six-thirty? We're going out to the Shire Horse Centre in the afternoon, but we'll be back by five. That'll give me

BLAIR CASTLE, BLAIR ATHOLL : J CAMPBELL KERR

time to give the children their tea and bath them before I change."

It was clear when I rang their doorbell, later that day, that they weren't ready.

Sally was in the kitchen preparing Tom's supper, and Emily, over-excited and grubby, was munching a sandwich.

"Oh, Meg, thank goodness you've come. We've only just got in. On the way home a caravan overturned in front of us! No-one was hurt but it was ages before they could sort out the traffic.

"I'm not anywhere near ready."

"That's all right, Sally. You go ahead and change, Emily will help me with Tom, won't you?"

Emily nodded happily, her mouth full.

I gave Tom his supper and heated some milk for Emily's drink. Then I bathed Tom whilst Emily played with the soapy bubbles in the bath.

Soon Tom was tucked up in his cot and Emily, looking pink and sweet, was sitting up in bed in her nightie, ready for me to tell her a story.

Just as I was about to start, Bill came in to kiss her goodnight.

"I want Grandad to listen, too," Emily insisted when I took her story book down from the shelf.

"Oh, but he's going out with Mummy and Daddy," I objected.

"They're not ready yet, Meg," Bill said, "but I won't stay if you'd rather I didn't."

"Meg doesn't mind," Emily told him. "She tells stories to *hundreds* of us at the nursery!"

So there I sat, with Emily snuggled up to me, and Bill seated on a chair and smiling at us both.

I kept my voice steady, but I could feel the colour stain my cheeks. I was annoyed with myself, behaving like a schoolgirl!

At the end of the story, Sally and Richard came in to kiss Emily goodnight. Then her grandfather kissed her, too.

"Now you must kiss Meg," Emily instructed bossily.

Bill leaned down to kiss me gently on the top of my head.

"I loved the story," he murmured before leaving the room quickly.

◀ *p103.*

BLAIR CASTLE, PERTHSHIRE

*T*HIS *is the seat of the Duke of Atholl, the only man in Britain allowed to have a private army, the Atholl Highlanders. Part of the castle was built in 1267, although only traces of that now remain. The area abounds in climbs and walks, particularly the track through Glen Tilt to Braemar, explored by Queen Victoria.*

"That was a really, really nice story," said Emily as she yawned into the bedclothes, "and it had a lovely happy ending."

THE days that followed were really good fun. Emily made it clear that she wanted me to be included in the family outings and Sally was glad of the extra pair of hands to help with the children!

I was included in the trip on the top of the double-decker bus, we saw the zoo, went on a nature trail, visited the local play park and even travelled on an old-fashioned steam train.

One lovely afternoon Bill suggested a game of tennis at the local tennis court and, with Emily as our ball girl, we enjoyed a gentle game.

All too soon it was Bill's last day and in the evening he took me out to a smart restaurant for a meal.

I'd had my hair done and put on my favourite blue dress. A little discreet make-up and an opal pendant completed my look.

I'd promised to say goodnight to Emily before going out and found her tucked up in bed.

"Oh," she breathed, "you look like a fairy godmother."

She looked at me thoughtfully.

"I must speak to Grandad," she said seriously.

"But you've said goodnight to him already," said Sally.

"Yes, I know, but I want to say something to him."

Whilst Bill went upstairs to hear what Emily had to say, Sally and I had a glass of sherry together.

"You look great, Meg," Sally told me kindly and kissed me lightly on the cheek. "Have a great time," she said as Bill escorted me out of the house.

The food was delicious, the dining-room elegant. A pianist was playing quietly at a grand piano at the end of the room and the atmosphere was very romantic.

Bill took both my hands in his and my heart began to thump.

"Meg, I know it's only a few weeks since we met, but I feel that I've known you for a long, long, long time, as Emily would say.

"These weeks together have been such fun and made me realise that, although I have a successful business and a lovely home, I've been lonely on my own.

"We seem to have so much in common . . . I've grown to love you, Meg — oh, I'm no good at speeches," he finished unhappily. He paused, then took a deep breath.

"Emily wants you to be her real gran. Oh, Meg will you marry me?" he asked softly, his gentle eyes tender.

Tears of happiness came into my eyes.

"Bill, if it's all right with Emily, then it's more than all right with me!" I smiled.

Bill's face lit up in delight.

"Is that a yes?"

"Yes, it is," I told him earnestly and this time I didn't blush when he kissed me! □

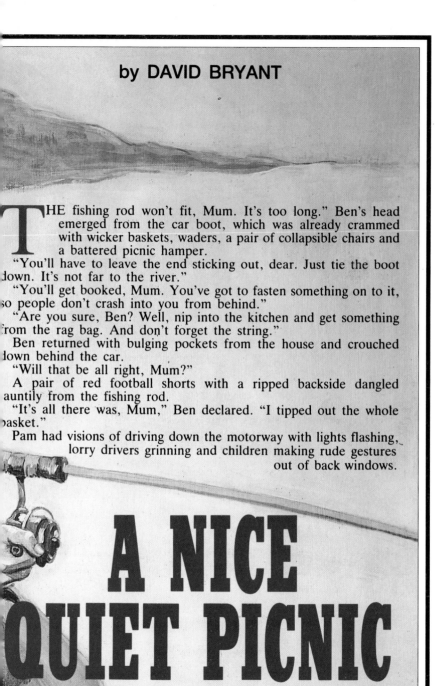

by DAVID BRYANT

THE fishing rod won't fit, Mum. It's too long." Ben's head emerged from the car boot, which was already crammed with wicker baskets, waders, a pair of collapsible chairs and a battered picnic hamper.

"You'll have to leave the end sticking out, dear. Just tie the boot down. It's not far to the river."

"You'll get booked, Mum. You've got to fasten something on to it, so people don't crash into you from behind."

"Are you sure, Ben? Well, nip into the kitchen and get something from the rag bag. And don't forget the string."

Ben returned with bulging pockets from the house and crouched down behind the car.

"Will that be all right, Mum?"

A pair of red football shorts with a ripped backside dangled jauntily from the fishing rod.

"It's all there was, Mum," Ben declared. "I tipped out the whole basket."

Pam had visions of driving down the motorway with lights flashing, lorry drivers grinning and children making rude gestures out of back windows.

A NICE QUIET PICNIC

Oh well, she thought, let them. Life's too short to worry.

"Everything in, Ben?"

"Yep. I've put the maggots in the front pocket. Next to your handbag."

Pam gave an involuntary shudder, and tried to put them out of her mind.

"Right," she said cheerfully. "Off we go."

She was over-optimistic. The ancient car wheezed, vibrated and gave a cough like a dying duck.

"Oh, Mum," came a voice from the back. "This car's a heap." Ben waited till the self-starter had cut off.

"There's a secondhand Porsche for sale at the garage, Mum. It's only ten grand."

Only ten grand! Since Bill had died in a tragic accident at work a year ago, Pam had been hard pushed to pay the bills and keep Ben in clothes. Already his feet were like dinner plates.

"Don't worry, Ben. Mr Crossman from next door showed me what to do."

She jumped out, opened the bonnet and took two loosely hanging wires between her fingers.

"You just join these and it'll start," she said, and touched the wires togther gingerly. There was a fizz, a blue flash and a faint smell of burning. She gave a scream.

"Are you all right, Mum?" Ben tried to keep the smile off his face.

"Fine," she said. "I must have picked up the wrong wires."

Five minutes later, they were heading out of Sturcombe on to the main road.

The engine chose a convenient spot to die, just beside a bus lay-by.

"We'll never get there at this rate, Mum. The fish will have died of old age by the time we turn up."

Ben had a point.

She watched cars whizzing past in their hundreds. Nobody seemed the slightest bit interested. How could she attract attention?

Then she had a brilliant idea. She opened the door and squeezed herself along the side of the car, trying not to notice the lorries thundering by.

The football shorts were still there. She undid the string, gave them a good shake and took her place at the side of the road, holding them above her head and waving them like Britannia flaunting her trident.

Ben curled up into the back seat, his face scarlet with embarrassment. Mothers! They were the absolute end!

IT had an instant effect. Cars started blaring their horns. Lorry drivers shouted and gave her the thumbs-up sign. A startled motor-cyclist narrowly missed running into the emergency telephone booth.

"Please stop!" she muttered, eyeing a well-dressed party in a brand-new Mercedes, but they didn't.

It was an ancient Land-Rover that swerved into the lay-by, drawing to a stop just in front of her. From the back emerged squealing noises and an appalling smell.

The Land-Rover door flew open, and a tall, slightly stooped figure of about thirty-five emerged. He was wearing a floppy green cap, an ancient tweed jacket, a pair of muddy moleskin trousers and wellies. He had to be a pig farmer on the way to market.

"Funny place to cheer your team from," he said jokingly.

"Very funny," she said drily. "Actually, I'm trying to take my son fishing. We've broken down."

He grinned.

"Well, I'm no mechanic, I'm afraid, but I do know the lad who runs the garage in the next village. Would a tow be any help?"

"What do I have to do?" She looked doubtful. "I've never been towed before."

"Just steer," he said cheerfully, "and brake when you see my lights come on. There's nothing to it."

"Are you sure it's no trouble?"

"None whatsoever." He disappeared into the Land-Rover and came out holding coils of oily-looking rope. Then he lay down on the ground and squirmed under the car.

She stood looking down at the soles of his boots and listening to the grunts coming from beneath the vehicles.

He wriggled out, wiped the oil off his face with his cuff, and pushed the cap back to a jaunty angle.

"All systems go." He smiled. "And don't forget to put the pants back!"

It was a bit weird at first. The steering felt wobbly and the car swayed from side to side. Pam soon got the hang of it and had just started to whistle the first bars of "Oh, What A Beautiful Morning", when there was a jerk and the Land-Rover began to disappear up the road ahead of her.

"The rope's broken, Mum."

"I had noticed," she said, watching the line of traffic building up behind. Their speed dropped from 50 to 40 . . . to 30 . . . to 20. An enormous lorry thundered past, shaving the paintwork off her door.

She saw it at the last minute, a narrow slip road. She swung the car off to the left, and began to glide gently down a steep hill. She manoeuvred round several sharp bends, and wonder of wonders, rounded a corner to find herself alongside a delectable stretch of river.

It was surrounded by weeping willows with grass banks sweeping down to the water. A perfect spot for a picnic.

"We've arrived," she said triumphantly. "A picnic site for the Queen, and you've got your fishing."

"You're a genius, Mum." She tried to ignore the sarcasm in Ben's voice.

They unpacked the fishing gear, took out the car rug and the chairs, hoisted up the picnic hamper and strolled down to the water's

THE FARMER AND HIS WIFE

by John Taylor

"JOHN, where were we thirty years ago today?"

We were sitting at the stove. I noticed that Anne had dropped her knitting on to her lap and was looking into space. I guessed she wasn't looking at anything in particular, but she was thinking a lot.

It was the third Tuesday in February, a cold, miserable day with a wind blowing across the Riggin.

Anne said I should remember as the weather was the same thirty years ago that day.

"We were at Uncle Jim's funeral."

On my arm, Aunt Mabel went to take her place in the front pew in Crail church. Anne followed and sat beside her in the pew.

Despite the weather, it was one of the best-attended funerals in that church for years. The farming community came to pay their respects to a great couple.

Anne and I owe more than we can ever repay to "Uncle" Jim and "Aunt" Mabel.

If it hadn't been for Uncle Jim we might well have never got married.

The year was 1932. I kept Old English Game bantams.

A stone-mason came to repair some of Dad's dykes. He saw my bantams and said, "Boy, that one's a show winner."

Neither I nor Dad knew till then that he was a breeder and judge of bantams.

"Put it in Cupar Show, boy."

I was excited — I owned a prize-winning bantam!

edge and made themselves comfortable.

"You can do a bit of fishing till lunchtime," Pam said happily.

"There's just one thing you've forgotten, Mum." His voice sounded ominous.

"What's that, Ben?"

He picked up the fishing reel and pointed it in the direction of a gleaming notice board.

"No Fishing. How am I supposed to fish with that stuck there?"

"Like this!" She rummaged in the back of the car, found the football shorts and hung them over half of the notice, obscuring the NO.

"Nobody will be any the wiser," she said cheerfully. "Passers-by will think you're a paid-up member of the local fishing club."

She had just started chapter one of her library book when a shadow fell across the page.

THE man was huge. He was wearing a deerstalker hat, plus-fours and heavy boots and had a shotgun tucked under his arm.

Out of the corner of her eye, she saw Ben trying to hide his fishing rod under a blackberry bush. She gave the giant a sweet smile.

T was duly entered for Cupar Show, and on the morning of the show I took it at 8 a.m. nd had it caged for judging.

The tent was to open at 10 a.m. for the ublic and entrants like me to see the judges' eliberations. It was the longest two hours of y life.

I've always been interested in sheep, so to ut off time I made for the sheep-pens. Pens three black-faced lambs were being judged, nd one had been awarded first prize.

"Hello, John," a voice hailed me.

It was Jim, a farmer from Crail who was a reat friend of my dad's.

I was anxious to learn and asked Jim, "Why d that pen get the first prize?"

We walked round to it.

"John, I'll tell you what to look for. John, ok at the bloom on those fleeces." He abbed one and parted the wool. "Look at eir straight backs."

Jim grabbed another. "Feel its back," he ged.

He put his huge hand across its back and ught me how to judge its weight.

"Look at that face, John, it's a clean face."

"Going to make me an offer, Jim?"

The owner of the pen had come across when he saw Jim taking such an interest in his winning pen. The two shook hands.

"Nae, not this week, Ian. John here wanted to know why you got first prize. I was showing him why."

"Laddie," Ian said, "you're lucky to be getting a stock judging lesson from the best stockman in the East Neuk."

Looking back, I learned more in those few minutes from that practical demonstration — with years of experience behind it — than I could ever have done from any textbook.

I TOLD Jim I had to get back to the poultry tent to look for my prize bantams. I didn't mention a prize to him — it was only in my mind.

As I left he invited me to his farm.

"Come over for a bite. Mabel would be pleased. We'll wander round the stock after."

I thanked him, and little did I realise, why and how soon I would be taking up his invitation.

The poultry tent was full, judging had finished. I expected to see a red, first-class ticket on the cage of my wee hen.

Through the bars of the cage was a "Highly Commended" ticket. My world fell apart!

"Lovely day," she said. "Just the spot for a bit of fishing and a picnic."

He stumped across to the notice and lifted the shorts off with the gun barrel.

"Can't you read?" he growled. "This is Lord Downside's private estate and I'm the water bailiff." He eyed the banger disdainfully. "I'd like you to move this . . . car . . . right away."

"I can't," she said. "It's broken down."

"Broken down. That's all I need!"

Rescue came in the shape of the Land-Rover. It swayed and jerked down the lane, and pulled up. The farmer jumped out.

"Sorry about that. It was the rope. The oil must have rotted it.

"I had the devil of a job finding you. There wasn't a left turn for miles."

He caught sight of the other man in the blackberry bushes, where he had been sniffing out the fishing rod.

"Hello. Who's this? A friend from the fishing club?"

"It's the water-bailiff," she said. "He . . . er . . . would like us to move."

The water-bailiff bared his teeth and growled.

"Five minutes," he snarled. "I'll give you five minutes."

"Come on," the farmer said. "We don't seem too popular here. It's time we made a move." He gestured towards the Land-Rover.

"I can do much better than a picnic. The Old Cherry Tree Tea Rooms are just down the road. Be my guests." He put an arm round Ben's shoulder.

"What do you say to scones and cream followed by chocolate cake, young man?"

"I'm on." Ben grinned impudently. "It sounds much better than Mum's Spam sandwiches."

"It'd be a real treat," Pam said, and she meant it, too.

It was a marvellous meal; sandwiches, buns, scones, meringues and chocolate profiteroles. The farmer, whose name was Bill Smith, was great company.

He told them that he kept a pig farm, and was a leading light in the local Farmers' Club. Over the second cup of tea, he mentioned to Pam that he had lost his wife some years ago in a riding accident. His sister came in some days to help him keep house, but inevitably, he was lonely.

Ben was just working his way through a fourth scone and his third glass of ginger beer when Bill made a suggestion.

"How about showing the two of you over the farm? I've got some rare black and white sows that have just farrowed.

"And Ben would enjoy the goats. They're the Egyptian ones with long, floppy ears. You don't see many of them."

Pam wasn't sure. He glanced at her, and turned to Ben.

"There's a mill-pond on the farm, with some of the biggest tench in the country — and no water-bailiff!"

"What do you think, Ben?"

There was no need to ask. His face was eager.

"Tench, Mum! You can get real whoppers. Two feet long!"

"And I don't always smell of pigs." Bill cashed in on his advantage. "I've got quite a smart suit at home."

HALF an hour later, they left Ben happily fishing in the mill-pond at Quarters Farm, and went into the barn. It smelt of straw and leather and goats.

They leaned over the pen, watching the tiny Egyptian kids tottering around on uncertain feet.

"We used to make goats' cheese and sell the milk," Bill said. "It was always in great demand."

"Why don't you still do it?" she asked. "The delicatessen near us is always saying how difficult it is to get good local cheeses."

"The goats were Betty's interest," Bill said. "I kept the dairy side going for a while after her accident. But it just wasn't the same, somehow." He began to stroke the silken ears of the baby.

"To be honest, it kept bringing back the past too much."

"I'm sorry," she said gently. "I didn't mean to intrude."

"Don't worry." He smiled at her. "It's good to have somebody to talk to again. That's what I miss most." He threw a handful of straw to the goats.

"There's always something going on when you live on a farm. Lambs being born, a fresh litter of piglets, the first sowing of spring barley . . . but it's not the same when there's nobody to share it with."

Nobody to share things with! He had hit the nail on the head. There were so many things she had longed to share since Alan's death. Ben's football colours . . . Her birthday . . . school sports day . . .

The time she'd had a poem accepted by the local paper . . . the weekend she and Ben had spent in a caravan by the seaside . . .

And now, here she was, enjoying being with a man again, listening to his slow, deep voice, enjoying his companionship.

"I've been talking about myself much too much, Pam," he said, breaking in on her reverie. "What about you?"

She saw his eyes flicker to the wedding ring on her finger.

"There's just Ben and me," she said. "We've been on our own for nearly a year now."

"It must be very difficult for you bringing up the boy by yourself." He shook his head. "So many marriages seem to go wrong these days."

"No, Bill," she said quietly. "It isn't like that. Alan had an accident at work. He was killed instantly.

"I just keep telling myself he wouldn't have known anything about it . . . but it was a terrible time. Ben's just beginning to find an interest in life again. That's why I'm so pleased he's taken up fishing."

"And you?" he asked. "How are you coping, Pam?"

She managed a smile.

"Putting a brave face on it and keeping myself busy. It works, most of the time."

"And when it doesn't?"

"That's usually about three in the morning. I go downstairs and do some ironing, and then I go back to bed, curl up and cry myself to sleep."

He took his hand off the edge of the pen, and laid it gently on her wrist. It felt heavy and warm.

"I am sorry, Pam. Believe me, I am sorry."

At that moment the barn door burst open.

"Mum, look what I've caught!" Ben was excitedly holding aloft a tiny, grey fish. "It's all of a foot long, Mum. I had a real struggle to land it."

"It must be a good omen!" Bill grinned. "The story goes that my great-grandfather caught a giant, two-foot fish in the millpond, and the next morning he married and inherited Quarters Farm, all in twenty-four hours."

All too soon it was time to leave.

"Look, Pam. Next Thursday the Young Farmers are holding their

H

F LORA, having secured a pass for herself and her maid, dressed up the Prince as Betty-Burke, and in this disguise she managed to smuggle him across the Minch with four stalwart islemen pulling at the oars of an open boat. They landed at Kilbride in Trotternish, Isle Of Skye, on June 29. Flora then took him to Kingsburgh House, and the next day to Portree where they said goodbye. The Prince knelt and kissed her hand.

annual barn dance here. I suppose you and Ben wouldn't come along as my guests? It would mean a lot to me."

For a second she hesitated. Then she remembered the touch of his hand on hers, and the understanding in his voice when she had talked about Alan. It had been a real comfort to share his company.

It was the warm smile that decided her.

"I'd like that, Bill. I really would."

T HE barn was warm and cosy and full of people and laughter. A long table stretched its length, lit by turnip lanterns and spread with food. A group of fiddlers, dressed in nineteenth century clothes, was tuning up on a small stage.

Bill took her arm and led her across to a bench.

She felt heady and light, looking forward to the evening that lay ahead. She had spent so many nights in on her own. with Ben fast asleep and only the TV for company, that she had almost forgotten the delirious excitement of an evening out.

Ben slipped off and joined the party of youngsters who were climbing on the hay bales in the corner.

She watched him slide happily into the group, and relaxed. Ben, too, was beginning to lose the pale, withdrawn look that had haunted his face for months.

114

They sat down on a bench and watched the dancers. One young couple whizzed past at a dizzy speed, cavorting and twisting and laughing joyously in each other's faces, and the mood caught them.

"Come on." Bill took her arm. "Let's join in."

He was a good dancer, and she followed his lead, nervously at first, then with growing confidence.

Soon there was magic in the air. The glowing turnip lanterns, the warm smell of hay and the shadowed rafters and the happy crowd cast a spell on them.

They danced, and danced again, and the time seemed to pass in a blur. Ben came over only once during the evening, to ask for some pocket money. Then he was off again, leaving Pam and Bill to talk and laugh together as they slowly unravelled the strands of their lives.

Too soon, the fiddlers struck up the last waltz. The lanterns were blown out one by one, leaving only a faint glow of light in the barn.

The fiddlers changed to a low, warm rhythm, and Bill took her hand and put his arm round her and began to dance. Slowly he drew her closer until she could feel the warmth of his body and the powerful muscles of his chest as he held her.

Somewhere inside her she could feel a tingle of happiness stirring, and she wanted the dance to go on for ever.

For Bill, the old, empty world seemed light years ago. The smell of her hair, the softness of her body, and the wonderful intimate feeling that this evening was being shared with a woman, were whirling round in his head.

He turned his head slowly, looked at her bright eyes, and soft, full lips, and wondered whether he dared to kiss her.

She knew what was in his mind.

"Yes, Bill. Yes, please," she whispered.

At first the kiss was warm and gentle, and then it bcame a burning fire, and they both felt as if new life had been born in them.

The music died, the lights went on and the spell was broken.

"Mum!" Ben ran up to them. "One of the boys says there are bream in the river. Can we come again on Saturday?"

"Well, Ben, I rather think that depends on Bill," she said. "You'd better ask him."

"Can we, Bill? Go on. Say yes, please."

"Any time you like, Ben," he said. "And I'll tell you what. If you catch a two-footer, I'll give you five pounds. How about that?"

Ben, his face one broad grin, ran off to tell his new friend.

Bill turned to Pam and held her hand in his. "It's been a wonderful evening. I've enjoyed every moment."

"So have I," she said. "And thank you for giving me such a lovely time."

He put his hands on her shoulders and stood looking into her eyes.

"There's just one thing, Pam. Today's only Thursday. I don't know how I'm going to wait till Saturday to see you again."

Her eyes lit up and she smiled back, a deep, secret smile.

"I was just thinking the very same thing . . ." □

GABBY stood in the middle of her teenage daughter's bedroom, a smile playing on her lips. Her gaze strayed to the walls, covered with faded posters of pop stars who'd long ago fallen from favour. Yes, Sam would think her birthday surprise *cool*, to use her current saying.

She and Sam had returned to her mother's house in Guernsey three years ago, shortly after her divorce. At first, making the move from London had seemed an irrational decision.

Her friends had been against it, but nothing they could say or do could ease the heartache, and nothing could change the fact that

A NEW BEGINNING

Peter had left her for his secretary.

Gabby pushed aside the past and focused her thoughts on the present. What mattered now was re-decorating her daughter's room before she returned at the weekend.

"Any sign of Mr Anderson?"

**by
LORI
DUFFY**

Her mother, dressed in a green dress with splashes of pinkish flowers, came into the sunny room.

Gabby shook her head. "Not yet, Mother. He did say he'd have a busy work schedule this week."

She suppressed a smile as she watched her mother studying the poster of a young, leather-jacketed youth astride a motor-cycle.

"You'd think he'd have made the effort to shave before having his photograph taken," Mrs Richards said, making a clucking noise. "Whatever do young girls see in scruffy young men like him?"

"Probably the same thing your generation saw in Errol Flynn," Gabby replied. "And mine in Kevin Costner."

"Who, dear?"

Gabby was about to reply when a voice from the doorway interrupted, "You didn't tell me you had a crush on Kevin Costner, Mum!"

Gabby smiled at the sight of the tall, blonde-haired girl in the doorway. Sam dropped her bags to throw herself into her mother's arms.

"Hi!" She hugged Gabby. "I've missed you. And you, too, Gran," she called over Gabby's shoulder.

"We've both missed you." Gabby pulled back to view the hold-alls. "What's going on? You're not due home until Sunday."

Sam shrugged. "Pam's got a new boyfriend. And three's a crowd."

"So much for our surprise," Mrs Richards murmured.

"Surprise? What surprise?" Sam flashed a grin that transformed her pleasant expression into a gleam of impishness. "And what are you two doing in my bedroom?"

"We were planning to redecorate it," Gabby admitted with slight disappointment. "You must have described Pam's bedroom to us at least a hundred times, maybe more."

"Mr Anderson's coming today to change the wallpaper and freshen up the paintwork. It'll only take a couple of days, then we'll all go into town and you can choose a new duvet cover and curtains," Mrs Richards added.

"I've changed my mind about Pam's bedroom — and about Pam," Sam announced.

Gabby and her mother exchanged worried glances as Sam added, "Thanks for the thought, but I'd prefer my room the way it is."

Gabby put her arm around her daughter's shoulders. "Go downstairs and make us all a pot of tea, darling."

After Sam had gone, Mrs Richards turned to Gabby and shook her head. "Why is it I feel as if I've just found a penny and lost a sixpence?"

TWENTY minutes later a van pulled into the driveway. Gabby held her breath as Sam went out to tell Mr Anderson she wouldn't be needing his services.

"Was he very upset, dear?" Mrs Richards asked on her return. "I suppose he gave you a tongue-lashing for wasting his time."

"I've changed my mind," Sam said cheerfully. "I do want my room decorated. Oh, and the painter wants to see you, Mum."

"Anything else I should know?" Gabby asked, getting up from the kitchen table. "You're looking at me the way you do whenever you want a special favour."

"Well, there is one other thing, Mum. Please would you ask if I could help out?"

Gabby wondered what had prompted her daughter's sudden change of heart. She didn't have long to wonder.

Pulling open the back door she let out a gasp of surprise. The man looking down at her was huge — he towered over her five foot ten, and he was also a complete stranger.

"You're not Mr Anderson," she said, finally finding her voice.

He thrust the paint-brush he was holding into the pocket of his white overalls and held out his hand. "Sean Holt, at your service. I'm Mr Anderson's nephew.

"I'm afraid my uncle's still finishing Mrs Symington's nursery. The baby came a few days early and now the room's got to be ready for tomorrow."

Gabby smiled and shook his hand. "Gabby Richards. Nice to meet you."

He had wind-tousled dark hair, a deep tan and dark brown eyes, and his soft, lilting accent told her that he was Irish. She felt her heart flip oddly as she looked up at him.

"That's Mark Douglas. He's working with us until college starts in the autumn."

Gabby looked past him to see a young man of about Sam's age coming up the path, several rolls of wallpaper in his arms. She grimaced quietly at the shock of thick, curly black hair that reached almost to his shoulders. Instinctively, she knew he was the reason for Sam's change of heart.

"Right. I'll show you to the room and let you get started." Gabby hesitated then added, "And I'll make some coffee."

Sean Holt smiled appreciatively. "Thank you, that's most considerate."

"I was wondering, Mr Holt," Gabby began, remembering Sam's plea. "Actually my daughter was wondering if she might help out."

Sean glanced back at Mark and nodded. "We'd be glad of an extra pair of hands, wouldn't we?"

Mark's eyes brightened. "Yes, most definitely."

Three hours later, Sam reluctantly came downstairs.

"I'm not hungry, Mum," she said, jutting out her chin stubbornly. "Besides, I promised I'd have lunch with Mark in half an hour."

"Mark?"

"He's studying to be an engineer," she went on, her eyes going soft. "And he's a big fan of Wet, Wet, Wet."

How can I argue with that? Gabby asked herself.

"Well then, perhaps you'd better ask Mr Holt if he'd care to join your grandmother and me for lunch — unless you intend taking him with you to the burger bar."

Sam gave her a puzzled smile. "How did you know we'll be going there?"

"A mother's intuition," Gabby said with a grin.

T HIS is very kind of you, ladies," Sean said, pulling out a chair and sitting at the kitchen table. "I'm sure it'll taste as good as it smells."

Odd, Gabby thought. Perhaps it was the way his brown eyes warmed when he talked or his gentle, vibrant voice, but she felt utterly comfortable with this stranger, even though they'd just met.

She tried to maintain a poised facade, but felt Sean's intense gaze. When her deep green eyes met his, she was surprised by the obvious appreciation in them.

"I do hope you like turkey salad, Mr Holt." Mrs Richards set a generously-piled plate in front of him. "My daughter's always counting calories."

Gabby blushed and skilfully changed the subject. "Thanks for letting Sam help. She's at a bit of a loose end."

Sean glanced across and grinned as if reading her thoughts.

"Mark's hair's a touch long, but he's a sensible young man," he said reassuringly.

Sean ate the meal with genuine enthusiasm, finally dabbing his lips with a napkin. "Mrs Richards, you're a wonderful cook. That was delicious."

Mrs Richards' face lit up at the compliment.

"What puzzles me is why teenagers prefer burgers to wholesome food. I would think they'd get sick of them eventually," Sean commented.

Gabby laughed. "I'm afraid not — better a burger made by someone else than a gourmet meal made by me."

They all laughed.

"My daughter, Gabrielle, is too modest, Mr Holt. She's an excellent cook. Her speciality is Italian food," Mrs Richards explained proudly. "Her zabaglione is heavenly."

"It's passable." Gabby was blushing again. "Mother, I'm sure Mr Holt isn't interested in my culinary skills."

She was rewarded with a grin. "On the contrary. My own cooking ability is somewhat limited. I seem to exist on frozen meals for one and restaurant food."

"You live alone?" Mrs Richards asked, ignoring the warning glance her daughter sent her.

"Yes, I do," he said. Amusement flickering in his eyes, he pulled himself to his feet. "Now then, ladies, I'd better get back to work. Thanks again for lunch."

After he'd gone upstairs, Mrs Richards stood, hands on her hips, looking at Gabby. Gabby thought she was about to offer some

"On Such A Night . . ."

O N such a night, I do not
    disbelieve
The stories told at ceilidhs round
    the fire —
The stars a net of old enchantment
    weave,
And voices haunt deserted croft
    and byre.
Now sails the moon, a Viking
    galley bold,
Beyond a sea of cloud, and longing
    fills
The heart with hunger for the days
    of old
When heroes walked among the
    hoary hills.

On such a night, brave Diarmaid
    might elope
With Fingal's bride, or fisherman
    ensnare
A mermaid in his nets, or scarlet rope
Restrain a Kelpie from his watery
    lair . . .
Away, you cynics! I will stay behind
To hear the harp of Ossian on the
    wind!

            — Brenda G. Macrow.

proverbial advice about the comforts of a husband in old age. Instead, she said simply, "I have to admit he's good-looking."

"Forget it, Mother, I'm not interested. Men are like flowers, strictly for admiring."

Her mother smiled, her cornflower eyes sparkling. "If you think looking at a man like that is enough, you've been working too hard. The right man can make it all worthwhile."

"He's pretty taken with you, Mum." Sam strolled into the kitchen, munching an apple. "And I think he's cool for an old guy."

"I don't think it's any of your concern," Gabby said. "And I wouldn't let Mr Holt hear you calling him an old guy — he can't be more than thirty-five."

"Just trying to help. You're not going to be young for ever, you know," Sam pronounced with an air of authority.

Gabby grinned. "I'm delighted you think I have a few years left."

B Y the weekend Sam's bedroom was unrecognisable. The walls were decorated in pale pink, the woodwork white, and at the windows hung curtains of delicate, bone-coloured lace.

Each day Gabby and her mother invited Sean to lunch with them in the sunny, spacious kitchen, and each day she listened earnestly while he laughed and offered titbits of his own life. She felt the familiar leap in her pulse at the pleasure of just being with him, and scolded herself for acting like an adolescent.

On the last day, Sam and Mark loaded the van. Mrs Richards was visiting a neighbour.

Gabby glanced towards Sean, standing in the sunlight pouring through the kitchen window. Nervousness rippled through her.

"Do you have time for a last cup of coffee, Sean?" she asked, folding a dish-towel. "I'm sure Mark and his helper can manage without you."

"I think they're counting on it." He smiled slowly. "I'd love a coffee, Gabby."

"Sam's delighted with her room," she said as she filled two mugs with the dark brew. "I can't tell you how much I appreciate it. She's even decided not to cover the wallpaper with those ghastly posters."

"I know."

Gabby looked at him. "You do?"

He shrugged self-consciously. "Apparently, I'm cool for an old guy."

"Right," Gabby said, wondering what else Sam had chosen to tell him.

"Sam knows how you feel about her wanting to spend Christmas with her father. She feels mixed up about it because she loves you both," Sean went on softly. "Don't be too hard on her, Gabby. She needed someone to talk to and I happened to be there."

Gabby nodded. How many times had she tried to talk to Sam about her father?

"I'd never stop Sam seeing him, Sean," she said finally. "She knows that and she doesn't blame you for your marriage break-up. She told me she understands that her father wasn't the ideal husband."

Sean took a sip of his coffee. "As for confiding in me, it's refreshing to know that despite all that's happened to her she still has the ability to trust."

"I lost mine with Peter." Her eyes darkened. "But then I suppose Sam's told you."

"Did he —" Sean asked, floundering for a polite way to put the question.

Gabby laughed without bitterness.

"Yes," she filled in for him. "He left me for his secretary. The thing that struck me later was that my friends all knew. I felt like such a fool."

"I had a rotten marriage, too." For a brief span, sadness flitted over his face.

"You seem to have a gift when it comes to dealing with teenagers. Do you have any of your own?" Gabby asked softly.

"About thirty." He paused for a moment, then sighed. "Or rather I did have."

Gabby gave him a puzzled smile. "I don't understand."

"Emulsion and gloss aren't my usual painting materials, Gabby. I used to teach Art at a college in Dublin." His mouth quirked as he remembered. "Not all of my students gave me an easy time, but I've always had a soft spot for teenagers."

"Do you still paint?"

"Apart from woodwork?" He nodded. "Yes. The tourists seem to like my seascapes and harbour views. I came to St Peter Port after my divorce intending to stay for a few weeks — and I never got round to leaving.

"I owe my sanity to Uncle Simon. Without him I don't know what I'd have done. Helping him when he gets a bit overworked is my way of thanking him."

Gabby said nothing as Sean was lost in thought. Instead, she was thankful for the opportunity to look at him one last time.

"Sorry." He glanced up at Gabby. "I was in a world of my own there."

Sadly she watched him drain his mug and rinse it.

"I'd better check on the youngsters," he remarked.

"We'll miss you," Gabby said quietly, unable to admit it would be she who would miss him most.

A bittersweet smile touched his eyes. In such a short time, only three days, she had grown fond of this huge, gentle Irishman. An emptiness pinched her chest at the thought of never seeing him again.

THE sound of laughter drifted into the kitchen, and she saw Sam and Mark standing in the doorway. Her daughter's eyes were starry as she gazed at the youth who tangled his fingers with hers.

Part 7

FOR assisting the Prince's flight, Flora Macdonald was imprisoned in the Tower Of London. Happily, her imprisonment was fairly brief.

After a day on Raasay (which was almost devastated by Government troops) the Prince returned to Skye. Now we must follow his trail along the path from Sligachan through the Cuillins to Elgol on outer Loch Scavaig. Here he found boatmen to take him back to the mainland. But again there was no ship to take him to France, and he had once more to return to the comparative safety of the Central Highlands.

"Is there room for one more at dinner tonight?" Sam asked, exchanging glances with Sean.

Gabby saw the sparkle of mischief in her eyes and knew who the extra guest would be. For once she didn't object to Sam's matchmaking.

"I did say you could invite as many of your friends to dinner as you wish. After all, it's not every day a girl celebrates her sixteenth birthday," Gabby returned with a smile.

"Will you come, Sean?" Sam flashed a cheerful grin.

"Are you sure you don't mind?" Sean said to Gabby.

"Of course not." Gabby grinned. "Count yourself among the élite. Sam finds most people over the age of twenty boring beyond belief."

"She's sweet," he said simply, "but not nearly as sweet as her mother."

His eyes darkened, a solemn vow of trust and lasting happiness in their depths.

Gabby couildn't help the tiny flame of hope burning in her heart, or the feeling that her daughter's sixteenth birthday would be one she'd remember always. □

THE FARMER AND HIS WIFE

by John Taylor

"OH, Dad, wait a minute!"

We were just about to drive out of our daughter and son-in-law's farmyard after Sunday lunch when our Mary called us back.

She came running over with a large, plastic bag full of something. She opened the boot and plonked it down.

"Enjoy it, Dad."

Anne put the kettle on for a cup of tea as we entered our kitchen.

"John, did you bring in that parcel of Mary's?"

I went back to the car.

No wonder Mary didn't let us see her present — the bag was full of eight, plump, unplucked pigeons.

As Mary's farm grows grain, they are plagued with pigeons, so she and our son-in-law had organised a pigeon shoot to try to reduce their numbers before the barley was ready for harvest.

Anne and I went upstairs to get out of our Sunday clothes and put on our everyday gear. We sat down to our cup of tea feeling much more comfortable.

"JOHN, let's pluck those pigeons."

As they had to be plucked sometime, that Sunday evening was as good as any time.

We went across to the barn, sat on milking stools and plucked into two buckets.

As we were plucking, Anne, who has a better memory than I do, said I had promised to tell readers about the doo'cots (dovescotes in England) in Fife.

As a boy I kept fantail pigeons. Dad and I put a small barrel on a pole and made it into a pigeon cote. I've always been interested in pigeons, so here goes about Fife and its doo'cots.

In the Kingdom of Fife, there are still more doo'cots than in any other county in Scotland.

At the end of the 18th century there was a survey taken and it was found there were 360 doo'cots. As they are now looked upon as wee buildings of historic interest, a survey was made and the numbers are now about 80. Why so many doo'cots?

IN those far-off days, farming was primitive compared with present-day methods. The way of feeding cattle and sheep through the winter had not been discovered, and except for a few breeding or working animals, all livestock were killed off in October or November and the meat was salted down.

This meant that, until the following summer, except for rabbits or hares, the only available fresh meat was salted.

This was the reason why salt was such a valuable commodity in the Middle Ages.

Salted meat day after day must have been monotonous so, by keeping pigeons — not in pairs, like I did, but in their thousands — the owner of a doo'cot could be sure of having a change of diet.

Only lairds, perhaps the minister and substantial farmers were allowed to build doo'cots.

I remember reading an article on the Fife pigeons. The writer stated that they descended "like a plague of locusts" on the fields, stripping the crops bare.

AT the beginning of the 18th century, a farmer called Townsend grew turnips for winter feed for stock. Later he was christened "Townsend Turnip." Be that as it may, by growing this root crop, stock could be kept during the winter months, thereby providing fresh meat all the year round.

From that date the need to keep pigeons declined.

By the way, Anne made a casserole from four of Mary's pigeons and it was mouth-watering!

IT was like the old joke, night fell — thud! Well, autumn had fallen not so much with a thud but with a whoosh and it was there, all over the garden in wind-driven heaps.

Nell raised her eyes and looked at the trees and shrubs, and shuddered when she saw their poor, damp, bare branches. Somewhere beneath that carpet of brown and gold, her lawn was gasping for air.

The birdbath and pond were awash with leaves, and the path was treacherously covered.

Any other year and Nell would have been out there with the first leaf, rake in one hand,

"As Others See Us"

by TERESA ASHBY

broom in the other.

But this was the year of her knee replacement operation. It had been successful, but it meant that she had to take things easy for a while.

Commonsense told her she shouldn't go dashing out and try to clear up, but she did hate to see the garden looking so unkempt.

"Next year," she muttered to herself, "you won't get the better of me."

This time next year, so the surgeon said, she would be tripping the light fantastic, and her stick would be relegated to some forgotten corner in a dark cupboard.

Maybe it wouldn't hurt to clear up a little bit, she thought — just between the house and the clothes-line. She could lean on her stick and use the brush . . .

Outside, up to her ankles in leaves and with a crisp wind swirling around her legs, Nell wasn't so sure. What if she slipped and fell? Who would know?

The garden which she had once loved for its privacy could also be her undoing.

With tears stinging her eyes, she conceded defeat and returned to the warmth of the house.

She hated being so helpless — so useless!

"Think yourself lucky you had an operation, that it worked and that you'll soon be on the go again," she said, angry with herself for her lapse into self-pity.

THE doorbell rang. It was obviously someone who knew her, for they didn't ring again but waited patiently for her to get to the door.

It was young Janie Burrows from Number Four. She smiled, then looked down at Nell's leafy slippers and frowned.

"You haven't been gardening, have you?" she asked.

"Me? Of course not." Nell chuckled. "The doctor said I wasn't allowed."

"Hm." Janie pursed her lips and stepped inside.

Nell had good neighbours. They'd promised faithfully they'd keep an eye on her, and they were doing just that. Not a day passed that at least one of them didn't come to her door to ask if she wanted anything done.

Apart from asking for a little shopping, Nell preferred to say she was fine. They had enough to do with their own families, without worrying about her.

"I'm off to the shops and I wondered if you wanted anything?" Janie asked.

"I could do with some tea-bags," Nell said thoughtfully. "Oh, and I'm nearly out of sugar."

At that moment, Janie's little boy rushed in, crying his eyes out.

"Whatever have you done?" Janie cried, but it was perfectly obvious.

He'd fallen and taken the knee out of his dungarees. Fortunately, he wasn't hurt, but the dungarees were in a bad way.

"They were new on this morning," Janie cried in despair. "Now look at them! Oh, Daniel, you must be more careful."

"Take him home and change him, then drop them in to me," Nell said. "I'll soon fix them — good as new. I can sew a patch on . . ."

Nell had always been handy with a needle, and when she'd finished with Daniel's dungarees, she smiled her satisfaction. She'd put a blue and white striped patch over the knee, and had added trims to the pockets and hems in the same fabric.

She just hoped Daniel liked them — and Janie. They looked quite different. Doubts crowded in and she put the dungarees into a carrier bag.

ANY jobs you want doing, Mrs B?" cheerful Jack Bryant from Number Eight asked.

He'd been unemployed for two years, but liked to keep busy.

Nell could have asked him to clear up the leaves, but she knew from experience he'd refuse any payment, even though he was hard up.

"Times are hard for us all," he'd say. "Put your purse away, love."

"There's nothing, Jack," she said now.

"What about that leaking guttering?"

He ignored her protests and strode through to the back. He stepped out into the garden and nearly tripped over the broom she'd left outside.

"I've got someone coming to fix it," she said. "I need a new bit put in."

"Oh, right. Well, I could have done that for you, you know, love."

The wind gusted and blew his hair across his face. He pushed it back impatiently.

"I'd get it cut if I had any money . . ." he began, then laughed. "I'll have to start wearing it in a pony-tail if it gets much longer!"

"I can cut it for you," Nell offered. "I used to cut my husband's. I've got proper scissors and everything."

He looked doubtful, then smiled and nodded and stepped inside.

They had a nice chat as Nell snipped and trimmed. When she'd finished, she told Jack to look in the mirror.

His smiled vanished, his jaw dropped, then he turned to look at her.

He didn't like it! she thought. She'd certainly cut a lot off . . .

"It's — it's — I don't know what to say," he stammered.

"Why don't you just go!" Nell said crossly. "I want to have my lunch."

In the end, he gave her a hug, kissed her cheek and hurried off back home.

When Janie arrived with Nell's shopping, she took the dungarees out of the bag and her eyes widened.

"What have you done?" she cried. "They look completely different."

Nell shrank back. This wasn't her day at all!

"You'd better go," she said stiffly. "I'm about to have lunch."

S TILL spluttering, Janie allowed Nell to usher her out of the house just in time to see Olive Johnson, the church organist, breezing up the path.

"Good morning!" Olive boomed.

Nell felt her cheeks burn as Janie showed her the dungarees. She couldn't hear what was being said, but she was sure it must be something uncomplimentary.

"I've just seen Jack," Olive began when she reached Nell. "I was admiring his new haircut."

"Don't want to talk about it!" Nell snapped. "You'll have come for your cakes?"

"You did some for the church bazaar? Oh, good on you, Nell."

Nell opened her larder door and brought out two tins.

"I did something a bit different this year," Nell explained. "I had a bit more time, so . . ."

She opened the lids and Olive gasped.

"That one's a praline and coffee gateau, and the other is a devil's food cake."

"But your usual madeleines!" Olive cried. "Your fairy cakes!"

Ungrateful lot, Nell thought!

"Take them and go," Nell said, shoving both tins into Olive's arms. "Go on!"

"But, Nell —"

Nell didn't bother with lunch. She was far too angry to eat. If anyone else came knocking on her door, she just wouldn't answer.

She did her best, didn't she? Tried her hardest? And what thanks did she get? None at all.

All afternoon she watched Australian soaps, and simmered angrily. At four o'clock she closed the curtains so she wouldn't have to look out at that mess of a garden, and at five, she made herself an omelette.

She didn't watch "Neighbours." She was off neighbours at the moment.

Then, when she got to bed, she couldn't rest. She really was turning into a crochety, bad-tempered old woman, she thought. So what if Janie didn't like her repairs? She *had* got a little carried away with them, she admitted. More than a little, she'd got carried away a lot!

And poor Jack. His shoulder-length locks had gone in an instant, snippety-snip! There he was with a flat top, which suited him perfectly, but which obviously came as a shock when he looked in the mirror.

As for the two fancy cakes . . . Everyone knew that fairy cakes sold best at church bazaars. Who'd want to buy her fancy cakes?

It wasn't her fault she was bored, but she had no right to take it out on everyone else.

"I'm not getting up tomorrow," she said, turning off her alarm. "I'm going to stay in bed all day and not see or talk to anyone!"

NELL managed to stick to her guns until half past nine the next morning. She'd wakened at seven as she knew she would with or without the alarm, and had stayed right where she was.

By nine o'clock, she was itching to get out of bed. It didn't feel warm and comfy any more, but lumpy and hot.

At half past nine, she rose, put on her dressing-gown and went to open the bedroom curtains.

The sun rushed in, the lovely golden autumn sun, and she blinked, letting her eyes adjust to the light.

Then she looked down — and blinked again.

That was Janie, wasn't it? She was stuffing leaves in a bag and then plonking Daniel on top. The little boy was gleefully trampling them down. He was wearing his dungarees, his altered dungarees that Nell had been sure would have been relagated to the nearest dustbin.

Jack was raking the leaves into piles for Janie while Olive was bending over the pond, fishing out leaves with a net.

How dared they!

Nell started for the stairs, but she couldn't move as fast as she liked and by the time she reached the bottom, her anger had started to fade.

When she reached the kitchen, she put the kettle on and started to make hot drinks for them all for despite the sunshine, it wasn't a very warm day.

A Seat In The Sun

*A*LTHOUGH he's reached his
    four-score years — and seven
more beside —
Great-Grandad, in his own quiet way,
enjoys life's eventide.
His legs won't take him very far,
but on a lovely day
Down the garden path he'll go,
in his slow, measured way.

Leaning on two sturdy sticks,
no need for rush and tear,
He'll ease himself into the seat,
beside the rose-bush there,
And, with the sun upon his face,
uplifted to the sky,
He revels in the scent of flowers,
the song of birds nearby.

Sometimes, his old dog pads along —
a faithful pal is she —
To rest her head, so soft and warm,
against Great-Grandad's knee.
And gentle is the gnarled old hand
that reaches to caress
The silky, golden-gleaming ears of
his beloved Jess.

Upon the drowsy summer air,
there's such a sweet content,
A feeling of fulfilment, and a peace
that's heaven-sent.
Oh, who could ask for more than this,
when life's long race is run,
Than a garden with a little seat,
to daydream in the sun?

— Kathleen O'Farrell.

Then, when everything was ready, she went to the back door and called them in.

"Don't Daniel's dungarees look super?" Janie asked, beaming all over her face. "They're like the ones he really wanted, but which I couldn't afford! He's dead chuffed with them."

Daniel, grinning impishly, twirled round.

"I couldn't tell you yesterday how pleased I was," Janie went on. "I was just so . . . so touched."

"You really like them?" Nell whispered.

Jack kicked off his boots and left them outside. With a sheepish grin, he ran his fingers through his cropped hair.

"Megan loves it," he said, blushing. "And so do I. I was just expecting a short back and sides, but when I saw what you'd done . . . well!" He laughed. "I was struck dumb."

"You really like it?" Nell whispered.

Olive came in, gave Jack a hearty whack across his shoulders and bellowed with laughter.

"You should see the cakes Nell made for the bazaar. I'll bet they'll be first sold. People go mad for the fancies, you know. Anyone can make fairy cakes, but our Nell really excelled herself."

"You mean they were all right?" Nell asked.

She blinked and shook her head. Maybe she'd stayed in bed too long and was hearing things! Perhaps she was still there and this was all a dream.

JACK gave her a hug.

"Why didn't you tell us you wanted your garden cleared up?" he asked. "You daft old thing, you should have known we'd be happy to do it for you."

"But how did you —?" Nell said, more confused than ever. "How did you know the leaves were bothering me?"

"The leaves stuck to your slippers," Janie said.

"The broom you'd left in the garden," Jack added.

"Your bad temper," Olive declared. "I knew there had to be a good reason for it."

For a moment Nell looked cross, her lips tightened and her nose turned upwards, but then she saw the funny side. Yes, they all knew her, better than she knew herself.

She poured them all a cup of tea and a glass of milk for little Daniel, then with a wicked smile, she opened the larder door.

"You know that devil's food cake I made for the bazaar, Olive? Well, I made two, but one went a bit wrong — well, a lot wrong. Not everything I do turns out right, but it'll taste just as good."

And to cries of delight and murmurs of appreciation, Nell produced a glorious looking, if slightly lop-sided cake.

She had some celebrating to do — not least the fact that she had the best friends in the world.

Tripping the light fantastic would have to wait, for right now she was happy with things just the way they were. □

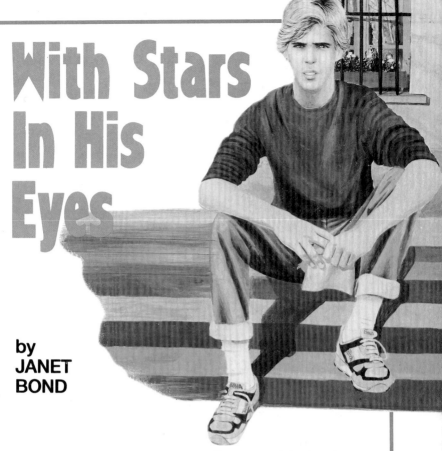

With Stars In His Eyes

by JANET BOND

"I'VE heard from Rory," Sheila ventured hesitantly as Jim finished his evening meal. "He wants me to meet him tomorrow morning in the shopping precinct."

She watched the colour drain from Jim's face. She felt it was only right to tell him. Yet, she hated shattering the calm that he'd managed to rebuild since their teenage son walked out, slamming the door on his family with devastating finality.

"In trouble is he?" answered Jim dryly. "Run out of money? Pop group folded?"

"He doesn't say." She fished in her cardigan pocket, then handed over the letter that had meant so much to her.

Jim tossed it aside.

"Surely you're not going? Not after all the worry and hassle he's caused us?"

"He's our only child, for pity's sake." A tear slid down Sheila's cheek.

"I don't want you to be hurt again, love." Jim reached across the dining table and squeezed her hand. "I just can't forgive Rory for not keeping in touch."

"He did, at first," Sheila countered defensively. "Well, with me, that is."

"And what happened?" Sarcasm edged Jim's tone. "Each time you met, he demanded money. And then, when their darned pop group finally took off . . ." He swallowed hard.

"You can't blame them for trying their luck abroad."

"Perhaps not. But the odd postcard wouldn't have gone amiss." Jim bit his lip. "No parent should have to chart their son's progress from obscure musical magazines."

"I wish he'd never set eyes on that wretched Duggie Barlow." Sheila sighed heavily.

Jim's eyes reflected her worry.

"You stay there," he said. "I'll make the coffee."

Sheila stared miserably into space, recalling the episode that had sparked off the rift between her husband and son.

"WHAT do you think of this, Dad?" Excitedly Rory held up the guitar he'd bought that afternoon with his savings.

"Half a mo." Jim laughed, dumping his coat. "Let me get in first." He kissed Sheila lightly, then sank down on the settee beside Rory. "Right. Let's have a look."

Like two peas in a pod, mused Sheila, comparing their bright eyes and animated features. Feeling almost like an outsider, she watched them admiring the instrument's polished body, taking turns to pluck its taut strings.

"I'm joining Duggie Barlow's new pop group," announced Rory gleefully. "He says I've got natural musical ability."

"Who's Duggie Barlow when he's at home?" Jim chuckled.

Sheila frowned and hurried off to dish up their meal. She was fed up hearing about Duggie Barlow. He lived a few streets away and was older than Rory. To her, he sounded flash, loud-mouthed and a born trouble-maker.

"Not your usual type of friend is he, Rory?" she'd asked earlier.

"S'pose not." He'd shrugged. "Music's all we've got in common." But the gleam in his eye spoke volumes as he'd added, "He's an absolute wizard on the guitar, Mum."

Long after dinner, Rory was still prattling on about Duggie's band.

"Practice sessions are on Tuesday and Thursday evenings," he told them.

"Those are your two worst nights for homework," Jim warned. "You can't afford to neglect your schoolwork, son. Especially with important exams coming up."

In a totally uncharacteristic outburst, Rory thumped the chair arm with his clenched fist.

"Exams! That's all you ever think about!" he yelled. Jumping to his feet, he faced them defiantly. "There's more to life than stupid exams."

Jim and Sheila stared at him.

"Who needs education?" he shouted, storming from the room. "I'm going to be a pop star, not an accountant."

"Don't give me that," Jim barked. He ran upstairs after Rory.

Sheila grimaced at the sound of their raised voices. Quarrels between her menfolk were rare, but when roused, both could be equally stubborn.

"We acted like a couple of idiots," Jim told her later. "We'll get over it."

But they didn't.

Sheila tried to ward off further memories of Rory's last few weeks at home. But it was no use. She could still picture her husband and son shaping up to each other, eyes flashing, faces contorted with rage. Snatches of their fiery exchanges rang vividly in her ears.

"Who needs school? Duggie says we'll be on the road soon, earning a fortune . . ."

"For goodness' sake, Rory. Get your priorities right . . . And while we're at it, must you wear your hair like that?"

"Duggie says it suits our image . . ."

Sheila winced. Torn between them, she'd tried hard to understand both and be a peacemaker. But in the end, it was Duggie Barlow's word that counted. The streetwise musician turned out to be a skilful manipulator.

D RINK this while it's hot, love." Jim's husky voice broke into Sheila's thoughts. She looked up to see him holding out a mug of steaming coffee.

Breathing in its rich aroma, she stared from the window at the dying rays of spring sunshine.

"I must go tomorrow, Jim. I need to see Rory," she stressed. "You do understand?"

Jim nodded. He sank down on the chair opposite and lapsed into silence, preoccupied with his own thoughts.

"Remember those awful jeans Rory wore?" He rolled his eyes heavenward. "The lurid T-shirts, the dreadful hairstyle?"

"All part of the image." Sheila forced a weak smile.

"Looking back, I suppose there were some humorous aspects." Jim's lips curved reluctantly.

"Mmmm." Sheila eyed his fading smile and pleaded, "Come with me tomorrow, Jim."

"What? When Rory's letter doesn't even give me a mention?" The hurt in his tone was unmistakable.

"It doesn't necessarily follow that he . . ."

"If he wants to see me, he can come to the house."

Sheila groaned in desperation.

"Can't you forget your silly pride for once?" she cried, her cheeks flaming. "OK, so he wanted to do his own thing. Does it have to ruin the rest of our lives? Couldn't you just . . .?" Her words petered out as she saw Jim's mouth tighten.

Mentally drained, she slumped over the dining table.

"Go to bed soon," he suggested kindly. "Get an early night."

SHEILA slept fitfully and woke with a strange sensation in the pit of her stomach.

Emotions in turmoil, she was simultaneously excited, apprehensive and a little afraid.

Jim was still asleep when she crept downstairs.

For a long while she stood hugging her dressing gown around her, staring at Rory's photo on top of the piano. It showed him fresh-faced, wholesome, and glowing with good health.

She wondered what sort of person he would be now. After almost two years on the road with Duggie and friends would he be foul-mouthed or covered with bizarre tattoos? Perhaps a tearaway with a weakness for alcohol? Heaven forbid!

Pushing her thoughts aside, Sheila studied her refletion in the hall mirror. Would Rory think she had changed? Did she look old for her forty years? Would he notice the worry lines etched on her forehead, the downward curve of her mouth?

In the kitchen, she forced down some toast. She tried reading but couldn't concentrate. She could think of nothing but the forthcoming reunion — or would it be confrontation?

Last time they'd met, Rory had been rather aggressive.

"Don't keep on," he'd snapped, angrily dismissing her plea to come home and make up with his father.

Sheila heard the stairs creak and looked up as Jim entered the kitchen.

"Bad night?" he asked, bleary-eyed. "Me too."

The atmosphere was strained and Sheila was glad of the excuse to go upstairs and get ready. She donned a flattering blue jump-suit and took great pains with her make-up.

At last it was time to leave.

"Come with me, Jim?" she begged, turning at the door.

Jim shook his head.

"Be careful, and don't let Rory take you for too much money."

Forty minutes later, Sheila was still pacing the precinct pavement. Checking her wristwatch for the umpteenth time, she craned her neck to peer anxiously through the jostling crowds of Saturday shoppers.

Had Rory been held up? Or had he changed his mind? I'll give him five more minutes, she vowed, knowing full well that she'd wait all day if necessary.

Coming suddenly from behind, his voice caught her off guard.

"Hello, Mum. Sorry I'm late."

Sheila's heart missed a beat. With a lump in her throat, she swung round.

"Rory," she breathed, falling into his open arms.

How long they stayed like that Sheila neither knew nor cared. It

On Bonnie Prince Charlie's Trail

Part 8

THE Prince's trail is now almost impossible to follow in detail. He slipped from glen to glen, and could be in Glen Affric one day, Glen Canness or Strath Glass the day after, or possibly moving by night high up on mountain slopes from which he could see the camp-fires of the Government troops far below. I have followed his steps through "The Window," a gap in the rugged hills of Corrie Ardair, Laggan.

He spent a week at "Cluny's Cage" — Cluny MacPherson's hideout on Ben Alder, above Loch Ericht — as well as many days in caves or on the open hill "soaked to the skin and devoured by midges."

At long last, a messenger came stealthily by night to tell him that a French ship was anchored near Arisaig, and this meant more desperate trudging over the hills and fording the rivers to get there in time.

He made it! He had been five months "on the run" since the defeat at Culloden. Happily, he now rejoined some of his friends, boarded the ship, and sailed for France.

only mattered that he'd shown up and wasn't ashamed to be seen hugging his mother in public.

Eventually she pushed him away.

"Let me look at you." Standing back, she dabbed her damp eyes and said emotionally, "You've grown so handsome."

She took in everything from his neat hairstyle to the sharp crease in his trousers. She fingered his crisp white shirt lovingly.

Then, they both spoke at once.

"Dad OK?" Rory inquired, whilst half-laughing, half-crying, Sheila asked, "What happened to the eye-catching gear and the way-out haircut?"

"It's a long story." He slipped a hand beneath Sheila's elbow and steered her away from the shops. "Let's go sit in the park and I'll tell you all about it."

They found a secluded seat near a flowering cherry tree. Each time the breeze showered them with pale pink petals, they laughed.

"I'm sorry, Mum," began Rory. "For everything. I soon realised what you and Dad had been trying to point out. But by then, it was too late. What an idiot I was — rowing with Dad — dropping out of

137

school and hurting you both."

"We all make mistakes," Sheila comforted him. "We probably nagged you too much."

She clutched Rory's hand tightly and listened whilst he spoke of the band's early gigs, when they were paid with beer and sandwiches. Only when pushed did he mention the bad days when there was neither food nor work . . . the long nights passed in freezing bus shelters and tube stations.

She sensed he was sparing her the worst.

"Our first break came when we sent a demo tape to this agent . . ."

Sheila's attention wandered. She was thinking crossly of the worry, of his birthday and Christmas spent apart from them.

"Why didn't you keep in touch?" she interrupted him.

"Pride," Rory explained. "I meant to. But somehow the longer I left it, the harder it became." He loosened his shirt collar. "Shame had a lot to do with it."

Red-faced, he drew an envelope from his jacket pocket.

"Cash," he said. "I owe you this. Some of it taken from your purse. The rest exhorted by . . . well, let's face it, Mum . . . emotional blackmail." Waving her protests aside, he opened her bag and thrust the envelope deep inside. "No arguments," he ordered.

Sheila's heart swelled with love and growing respect.

"The group hit it big in Holland," Rory said, returning to his story.

"We saw magazine pictures."

"Aw, Mum . . ." His smile was childlike. "Fame was great while it lasted."

"While it lasted?" Sheila echoed uncertainly.

He hunched his shoulders.

"The group's split up now and we're each going our separate ways. I've landed an office job with a London-based recording company. Nothing special, but at least I'm still in the music business."

"Well done . . . And Duggie Barlow?" she couldn't resist asking.

"He's starting afresh, recruiting more starry-eyed dreamers," Rory said wryly. "But, I'm fed up with the travelling. I feel like putting down roots again."

"London's not that far away . . ." She eyed him hopefully.

He laughed. "Don't worry, Mum. From now on we'll meet regularly."

Later, Sheila asked warily, "Will you walk me home?"

"Of course, but please don't expect me to come inside."

Her heart sank. So, he wasn't yet ready to face Jim.

Chatting non-stop they strolled back through the sunlit precinct. Sheila savoured every second spent in his company.

THEY'D covered half the distance when she spotted Jim coming towards them, probably on his way to the newsagent's.

Visualising a showdown, she panicked. What should she do? Warn Rory? Drag him into the nearest shop on some vague pretence?

She dithered. And suddenly, it was too late.

Jim had seen them and hesitated. Then, turning on his heel, he strode away.

Oblivious, Rory prattled on about some girl he'd been dating recently.

"I'm sure you'll like her, Mum. She's . . ." Startled by the sudden jab from Sheila's elbow, he broke off. Following her line of vision, he recognised his retreating father.

"Dad!" he yelled, breaking into a trot.

Sheila caught up and watched nervously as Jim slowed down. After what seemed an eternity, he turned to face them. She held her breath as the two men stared at each other. For an instant, the silence between them was overwhelming.

Rory backed off first.

"Friends, Dad?" He held out his hand.

"Friends," Jim agreed, grasping it eagerly. His face creased into a warm smile.

Next minute they were hugging each other, laughing and apologising all at the same time.

Tears glistening, fingers pressed to her mouth, Sheila listened to Rory telling Jim all about his new job.

"And guess what, Dad?" He sounded like a child trying to surprise. "I'm going to night school to get the exams I missed out on."

"Very wise," Jim nodded with obvious pride. "It pays to have some qualifications behind you."

Sheila finally managed to get a word in edgeways. "I've dreamed of this reunion for ages," she admitted. Ideally, it would have taken place at home where she could open the bottle of champagne she'd been keeping specially. "But I never imagined you two making up out here in the street, halfway . . ."

"What better place to meet than halfway?" quipped Rory, flashing his father a meaningful grin.

They all knew that Sheila had been going on to say 'halfway home'. But somehow, Rory's corny interpretation sounded so much nicer. □

A Prince Among Men

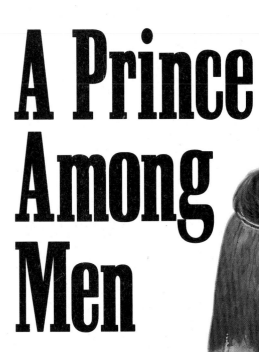

by PATRICIA A. SWIFT

JENNY took a deep breath as she tried to quell the rising tide of irritation inside her. Tony was late. It was already one-thirty.

That left only two hours before she had to collect Kim from big school, Amy from Nursery and little Jamie from Mrs McLeod, who would only baby-sit, "If you're really stuck, dear!"

She had two hours in which to drive into town and choose the dress.

"It's important," she'd insisted last night, when at last she'd flopped on to the sofa, exhausted after putting all three children to bed.

"I know, love," Tony had looked up from the pile of bills and VAT statements he was wading through. "I do understand. I'll be home in time."

His blue eyes had crinkled and he'd grinned teasingly.

frequent visits for morning coffee, "you're just like Cinderella, always the one who stays at home. You do let Tony make a doormat of you, don't you?"

"But I can't possibly go, Val," Jenny had explained, referring to the local operatic group's performance of "Iolanthe". "Tony has to work late every night next week to complete Mrs Walker's extension. It's the only way he'll get finished before she comes back from her holidays, and he did promise her."

Val had sighed. "And you're going to drop everything to stay in and look after the kids."

Jenny had shrugged before replying, "There's not much choice, is there? Someone has to stay in with them, and we can't afford a baby-sitter too often."

"But you always give in," Val had argued. "I mean, I know you would have enjoyed the Women's Meeting last month.

"We had a really entertaining speaker, but because Tony wanted to visit his mother in the nursing home you cancelled. He could have gone another night, you know."

"Yes," Jenny had had to concede. "But he'd already told her," she'd excused herself. "I didn't want to be the cause of her being disappointed."

"You're too soft for your own good," had been Val's reply. "Life's going to pass you by if you're not careful."

"Don't worry, Cinderella shall go to the ball."

Jenny had forced a laugh in return, but it wasn't really funny, she'd thought, because that was exactly how Val, her new friend, did see her — as Cinderella!

"Gosh, Jens," Val had said on one of her increasingly

L IFE certainly wasn't going to be allowed to pass Val by, Jenny had reflected later. Newly divorced, Val had moved into the cottage next door only three months ago.

"It's a bit of a comedown from Manor Park," she'd said looking around the small kitchen ruefully, when Jenny had gone round with tea and freshly-made scones after the removal men had left. "Still, at least I've got my independence now."

She'd smiled wryly.

"I'm campaigning to get on the local council," she'd confided. "What with the divorce and the move, I suppose I've had a bit of a set-back."

With a dismissive shrug she'd gone on, "Will you help me? You could introduce me to the people round here, widen my circle. I'm just going to throw myself into everything," she'd finished.

Jenny had nodded understandingly.

"Of course," she'd answered. "Of course I'll help."

"I do admire her," she'd told Tony later. "She's being so brave."

"Mmm . . . I suppose so," Tony had replied, "and it'll be nice for you to have a friend next door. Maybe she'll even baby-sit for us once in a while," he'd added hopefully.

But Val was much too busy for baby-sitting. There was canvassing to be done, leaflets, which Jenny had spent every spare moment stuffing into envelopes, to be pushed through letter-boxes.

Now it was all over and her friend was victorious.

"I'm so thrilled," Jenny had said hugging her.

"So am I!" Val's eyes had sparkled triumphantly. "And you must come to the dinner-dance with me to celebrate. I'll get your ticket, to thank you for all your help. You must come, Jens."

"But what will I wear?" Jenny had wailed to Tony when she'd told him about the invitation. "I'll have to look really good. There'll be all the bigwigs from the council there, and I can't let Val down. I don't want to look like the poor relation."

"You won't, love," Tony had said. "We can manage to afford you a dress. Blow the 'rainy day' — you'll have the most glamorous frock you've ever had, I promise.

"I'll leave work early on Tuesday and take you into town. You must go. Val's right — you don't get out enough."

H ERE she was ready and waiting, but there was no sign of Tony. The dinner-dance was now just over two weeks away.

If I don't get the dress soon, I won't be able to go, she was thinking as, at last, the blue van in which Tony transported his building materials appeared round the corner.

"You're late," she said accusingly when the van finally came to a standstill. "I'm never going to have time to choose something spec — "

"Jenny," Tony interrupted her, his face apologetic. "I'm sorry, love, but," he paused, "can we put off getting the dress today?

"I know how much it means to you but . . ." He let the sentence trail off and went to the back of the van.

"Look," he said, throwing open the doors. "I really had to do something about him."

Jenny walked to the back of the van, her heart sinking. There was no doubt about it — she knew she wasn't going to get the dress.

In the back of the van lay a huge dog. He was a mongrel and terribly thin. He had a long, shaggy, coat matted in places with drying blood. Two large, brown eyes regarded her beseechingly.

"He's been injured," Tony explained. "I found him lying by the side of the road. Some heartless driver must have hit him with their car and left him lying there.

"Jen — " Tony's face was full of pity and concern, his eyes tender, " — I couldn't leave him. He's in pain."

"No — " Jenny had to agree he couldn't have left him there, no decent person could.

"I'll have to take him to the vet," Tony was going on. "I'll have to use your dress money, just for now. But don't worry, I'll work extra hours at the weekend. I'll make it up to you. Jen, you'll have your dress in time for the dance, I promise you will."

"Well," Val said, breezing into Jenny's kitchen the next day. "Let's see it."

Jenny fiddled with the lid on the coffee jar.

"I didn't get it," she answered at last.

"Oh." Val sounded surprised. "But I saw you go out. You went a bit late, though. Was that it? You didn't have long enough?"

"No-o-o." Jenny abandoned the coffee. May as well get it over, she thought.

"Come on, I'll show you," she said resignedly. "It's in here."

She led the way into the utility room.

"There," she announced, flinging the door open. "Take a look at my new dress."

G OOD grief!" Val looked at the dog in consternation. "What on earth?"

"He's called Lucky," Jenny told her with thinly-veiled bitterness, "because the vet said he was lucky to be alive. If Tony hadn't come along when he did, and if Tony hadn't taken him to the vet immediately . . .

"Well — " she shrugged " — that's it, Val, that's where my new dress money went."

Val took a deep breath as she and the dog eyed each other. Lucky lay stretched out on a blanket, warm and cosy near the central heating boiler. For some reason he decided he didn't like Val much and gave a low growl.

"Well," Val said at last in a hollow voice, "I'm disappointed. I thought you really wanted to come to the dinner-dance. I thought for once you were going to put yourself first."

"I did, I do and I will," Jenny answered weakly, aware that the, "I will" was somewhat lacking in conviction. "I mean, Tony's promised

I'll get the dress. He's going to work overtime at the weekend to make up the money again."

Val wasn't convinced. "Couldn't you have taken it to a Dogs' Home or something?" she asked, regarding Lucky dubiously. "They would have fixed it up, wouldn't they?"

Jenny shrugged.

"Maybe they would, but Tony wouldn't abandon him," she explained. "Then the vet said he was going to need a lot of looking after."

"And you're going to do the looking after, as usual." Val sighed. "Well, how long will it be before he's better?"

"Not long," Jenny said. "The vet said with care he'll heal quickly. Be as right as rain quite soon."

"Then what?" Val queried. "You're not keeping the dog, are you?"

Jenny hesitated before replying.

"I don't know," she said at last. "Tony would like to, and the kids love him already."

"Oh, Jen, you're hopeless!" Val shook her head in despair. "With a dog to look after, as well as the kids, you'll have even less time for a life of your own."

Jenny made coffee for herself after Val had gone. I suppose it's no wonder she's disappointed in me, she thought dejectedly. I do seem to get bogged down in domesticity.

I'm in a rut — for ten years I've thought of nothing but Tony and the children. No wonder Val thinks I'm a doormat.

I'd even forgotten that I ought to have a life of my own.

Picking up her mug, she went into the utility room. Lucky's tail rose and fell in greeting.

"It's no use," she said, eyeing him sternly. "I'm very sorry, but this time it's going to be what I want, not what you or Tony or even the children want."

I WANT you to be happy," Tony said a week later, when he arrived back from the Dogs' Home. "Of course the kids are disappointed and, yes, I had grown fond of Lucky myself, but I realise I was being selfish.

"Anyway, not to worry — the people at the Home said they'd soon find him new owners. Now, love, I must rush if I want to get back for that overtime. Just this one more night and I'll have the money for that dress."

It was pale pink satin, dotted with old roses in a deeper colour.

"It's super!" Val beamed with approval. "The colour will really show off your blonde hair and the neckline's just right — sophisticated without being too daring."

Dark eyes alight with enthusiasm, Val hugged Jenny delightedly. "I'm so glad you're coming, Jen, so glad you're doing what you want at last."

Part 9

THE story of Bonnie Prince Charlie's exploits in Scotland were far from ended. The Highland folk had disdained all rewards for his capture, and had come to regard him as their "freedom fighter," especially so in the aftermath of Culloden when the Duke of Cumberland had no mercy on the clan folk, their villages or their way of life. Prisoners, too, were treated with great cruelty.

So it came about that a new folklore grew into being, and many songs were composed (by Lady Nairne and others) extolling the merits of the Prince, wishing and hoping he would return.

"Better lo'ed ye canna be,
Will ye no' come back again?"

And so the day of the dinner dance was here. Jenny paced the floor. What on earth had happened to Tony?

"I'll be in by four," he'd promised that morning at breakfast. "I'll see to the kids' tea while you have a long, luxurious bath and get ready for the dance."

But it was half-past! Oh, surely he wasn't going to let her down again.

The telephone rang. That'll be him, she thought as she rushed to lift the receiver. She didn't know whether to be angry at the delay, or relieved that he'd be telling her he'd be home in a few minutes.

"Hello," she said, keeping her voice neutral. But the voice on the other end wasn't Tony's. It was a Sister Mitchell from the local hospital — Tony had had an accident.

A gently smiling nurse led Jenny into the ward.

"He's going to be fine, Mrs Ferguson," she reassured her. "It's only a badly sprained ankle.

"We've X-rayed it, and there's nothing broken, but we want to keep him in overnight, just to check that the fall didn't do any other damage. You know, no concussion or anything. Then first thing in the morning you can come and collect him."

"Sweetheart, I'm so sorry," Tony greeted her.

"Shush." Jenny sat down by the bedside. "Don't apologise. You do look pale and tired, love."

"Oh, that's nothing," Tony brushed her comment aside. "Listen, Jen, it's you I'm so worried about — your dinner-dance. I don't want it ruined for you.

"You've still got time to get ready if you hurry. Promise me you'll go."

"Tony!" Jenny exclaimed, shocked. "I can't go now, not with you in hospital."

"But you must." Tony's expression became even more earnest and pleading. "Jen, if you don't go, I'll feel a hundred times worse. I fell because I was rushing. I desperately wanted to be home on time for you. It was so important to me that I didn't let you down.

"You see, I realise how much I've taken you for granted," he continued, his expression serious. "Val's right. I've assumed that because I'm happy with our life, you are. I'd forgotten that you deserve a life of your own, away from the kids now and again, that you need to do the things *you* want to do sometimes. Jen, please go to the dance, for my sake."

JENNY stood in front of the mirror thinking deeply. The dress fitted beautifully. Her hair was just right. The gold pendant Tony had bought her to celebrate their first wedding anniversary shone gently against her skin.

So why wasn't she happy? It wasn't that she felt guilty. Tony would be well looked after in the hospital.

Mrs McLeod had agreed that it was an emergency. "Yes, dear, I'll look after the children as a special favour, at such short notice."

There was nothing, nothing at all, to stop Jenny from going to the dance and enjoying herself just as Val wanted her to do, as Tony was insisting she did.

There was nothing to stop Cinderella from going to the ball.

The light from the bedside lamp cast a golden glow over the room. The dress she'd worn to the dance at which she'd met Tony had been shades of pink.

In this light I could still be that girl, she mused. Twenty years old she'd been, looking for romance, hoping for love.

That's what they'd all wanted, she and her friends, to love and be loved. It was what they'd all talked and dreamed about.

She stood silently in front of the full-length mirror for many moments, then slowly, but deliberately, she began to take off the dress.

"I'm not Cinderella, despite what Val thinks!" she exclaimed out loud, as the realisation came flooding over her.

She pulled on jeans and a sweater, thinking of Val. Val, was like a hard, bright diamond, and like a diamond she'd had the power to blind for a while.

Praying it wouldn't be too late, Jenny ran downstairs and outside to the van.

"You're lucky." The lady at the Dogs' Home laughed at her own joke as she handed Jenny the lead. "Someone nearly took him this afternoon."

"Yes," Jenny agreed, smiling, as she took Lucky out to the van, "I know I'm lucky. I just forgot for a while."

She settled the dog down on his blanket in the corner of the utility room.

"You'll be a nice surprise for Tony in the morning," she told him, then went upstairs to attend to the dress.

At first she'd thought of taking it back to the shop, then she'd decided not to. She'd keep it and wear it for Tony, but mostly she'd keep it to remind her of how hard Tony had worked for it, how hard he always worked for her and the children.

And it was so that she could be there, for the children, at least while they were young, for all of them, so that she didn't have to worry about, "a life of her own."

Val's voice on the other end of the phone was sharp.

"You aren't coming?" she repeated in disbelief.

"No," Jenny replied firmly, "I'm not."

She took a deep breath, then went on gently, "I'm sorry if I'm letting you down, Val, I really am, but it's not what you think.

"You see, I do have a life of my own, a life I chose. Tony and the children are my life, they're what I always wanted and still want.

"There's another thing, something we both forgot. I went to the ball, a long time ago, and just like Cinderella, I married a prince." □

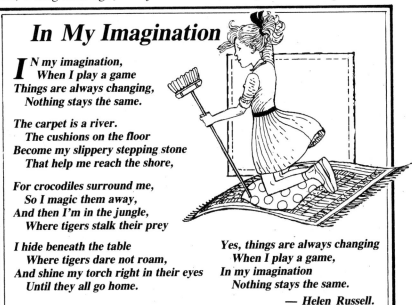

In My Imagination

*I*N my imagination,
When I play a game
Things are always changing,
Nothing stays the same.

The carpet is a river.
The cushions on the floor
Become my slippery stepping stone
That help me reach the shore,

For crocodiles surround me,
So I magic them away,
And then I'm in the jungle,
Where tigers stalk their prey

I hide beneath the table
Where tigers dare not roam,
And shine my torch right in their eyes
Until they all go home.

Yes, things are always changing
When I play a game,
In my imagination
Nothing stays the same.
— *Helen Russell.*

E XCUSE me, I wonder if it would be possible to —" The man who was holding a large, shrink-wrapped book on Flemish painting stopped mid-sentence and stared at her. "Good gracious, it's Anne, isn't it? Anne Cavendish?

"You probably don't remember me — Steve Anderson. I used to go out with your sister, Valerie."

"Of course, I remember you," Anne said truthfully.

Anyone would remember Steve Anderson. What was surprising was that he had recognised her after five years.

"Did you want to have a look at that book?" she went on. "Here —"

There was a small penknife attached to the ring of keys in her pocket. With the expertise of long practice, Anne slit the thin plastic that was used to protect the more expensive books.

She explained, "It's a nuisance, but with the price of some of these art books, we can't risk letting them get shop-soiled.

"A bookshop should be for looking at books, but the sad fact is that no-one is going to pay over twenty pounds for one that looks second-hand."

"Have you worked here long?" Steve stood with the book unopened in his hands.

"Three years. I did a secretarial course after school, and worked in a solicitor's office for

**by
GLORIA GAGHAN**

a year. I've always loved books, so when an opening came up at Warrener's, I jumped at it."

Steve's eyes took in the display tables and shelves. "You certainly have a good selection."

"Thank you. I'm the buyer now for the Art section. I'm also the assistant Floor Manager."

Anne was proud of her job in the city's largest and best-stocked book shop. The pay at Warrener's might not be as grand as her job description, but it was varied and interesting work.

"How about you?" she asked. "Have you been designing those buildings you used to dream about?"

Steve shook his head, smiling. "No, but I've become a dab hand at house extensions and garage conversions. Tell your parents that if they need an extra bedroom, I'm their man."

"I'm not living at home any more." Out of the corner of her eye, she saw one of her regular

FIVE
YEARS
ON...

customers waiting to be served. "Sorry, could you excuse me for a few minutes?"

The next time she looked over, Steve was at the cash desk, paying for the book. She watched him take the carrier bag with a tinge of regret. He hadn't changed much — still tall and lean, with almost Nordic colouring.

All Valerie's boyfriends had been good-looking, but Steve had that extra something to his personality that had made Anne's heart flutter privately and hopelessly when she was eighteen.

He caught her staring at him and walked back over, saying, "Look, I'd love to catch up on old times. When's your lunch break? Maybe we could have a sandwich together somewhere nearby?"

Her work as a buyer had taught Anne to make rapid decisions. She glanced at her watch. "There's a café just round the corner in Hanson Street. If you grab a table, I'll meet you there in ten minutes."

Valerie had been a fool to throw Steve over, Anne thought, as she ran a comb through her hair in the staff cloakroom. They'd made a wonderful looking couple, both so fair and blue-eyed.

But then, Val looked wonderful with anyone, and there was always a new boyfriend on the horizon, when the current one was deemed "too serious" or "too sporty" or simply "too boring".

"Valerie takes after me, and Anne takes after her father. Anne has his brain," Mrs Cavendish was fond of telling people.

She didn't have to explain that Val had inherited her blonde hair, porcelain complexion and delicate features, while Anne had got her father's brown hair, hazel eyes and an early need for glasses.

No-one meant to be unkind. Val couldn't help being the prettier child, any more than she could help being three years the elder. It wasn't her fault that people fussed over her, or that the clothes which were inevitably handed down over the years were chosen for a blonde, very feminine girl and not for a brown-haired tomboy.

Their father was a quiet man, absorbed in his work as a civil servant and a keen member of the local chess club. He'd paid for Val's dresses without demur, but he'd also found the money to buy Anne the books she loved, and had taken her to the zoo and the musuems.

Once, watching his wife brush out waist-length hair for a then fifteen-year-old Valerie, he'd said softly, "Did you know that originally the term 'to spoil' meant 'to destroy'?"

A S Anne had expected, the first question Steve asked after they'd settled with sandwiches and tea was, "And how's Val these days? Married, I suppose."

"No, not yet. She's living at home and working part-time at the local estate agent's."

Unlike Anne, Val had never had any proper training after school. Somehow everyone had assumed she would marry young, and that acquiring extra skills would be a waste of time and money.

"I'm sure the men are still swarming around, at any rate," Steve said, smiling.

"Of course."

But even as she said it, Anne realised that it wasn't quite true. Val was as beautiful as ever, but a lot of her old crowd had married, or moved on. On Anne's last few Sunday visits home, she'd sensed a restlessness in Val that was alien to her sister's normally placid and sweet nature.

"And what have you been doing yourself, Anne?" Steve asked politely. "Didn't you used to wear glasses?"

"I wore glasses for years, but I treated myself to contact lenses just after I started work. For the first few weeks, I felt as if I'd lost part of my face."

Anne smiled, then went on to describe her job, the evening class in French she was taking, and her tiny flat that was strategically positioned between the bookshop and the Polytechnic.

She added, "Dad hoped I'd go to university, but I wanted to get out into the real world. And I can still continue to study things that interest me."

Steve spoke of his own work as a very junior member of a large architectural firm, and how the slump in building had affected them. He was entertaining rather than bitter about his bread-and-butter projects, and full of enthusiasm for the future.

"One day, I'm going to find the most dismal, problem-ridden house in the city," he vowed. "Then with the help of my indomitable wife, I'm going to transform it, and everyone will say, 'But, my dear, you *must* use Steve Anderson. You should see what he did with his own home'."

"I didn't realise you were married."

Involuntarily, Anne looked at his ringless left hand.

"I'm not. The indomitable wife is part of the daydream." He grinned. "How about you? Anyone special in your life?"

"Not just at the moment," Anne replied.

In fact, her social life consisted of going out with a mixed group from the shop for a drink on Friday nights, occasional lunches with a woman from her French class, and fending off the attentions of a married sales representative from a large publishing firm.

They chatted on over a fresh pot of tea until it was time for Anne to return to work.

Outside the café, Steve paused indecisively, then asked, "Would you fancy going out for a meal or a film sometime?"

Anne meant to say no, but what emerged was, "That sounds nice."

They arranged to meet on Saturday evening.

Susan, from shop security, was a young woman whose brown eyes missed nothing. "Who was that gorgeous creature you were talking to?"

"An old boyfriend of my sister's. He asked me out. Do you think I should have accepted? I feel a bit funny about it."

THE FARMER AND HIS WIFE

NOWADAYS, friends often bring a gift of a bottle of wine or a box of chocolates when they come for an evening meal.

In the past it was something more down to earth and, if I may say so, more acceptable.

We'll never forget Alistair, a neighbouring farmer, and his wife coming. She handed Anne a guinea fowl, a very plump little bird.

Anne searched her cookery books for a recipe, and we really enjoyed that gift.

Alistair, or should I say his wife, Mary, bred guinea fowl for the Christmas market.

Anne bred turkeys for the same reason. She did well, but after two years she decided they were too much trouble.

The best watchmen round a farm are guinea fowl, turkeys and geese. If disturbed they set up an awful din and waken everyone.

One night, just before Christmas, someone decided to raid Anne's turkeys. The turkeys were in cages in the small paddock at the front of our farmhouse. The would-be thieves had not bargained for the noise the birds made when disturbed. They went away empty-handed, but what a problem we had at two o'clock in the morning trying to recover those birds!

WHAT made me think about gifts in the country was a request from Anne one morning in November over breakfast.

"John, get me two young rabbits, please. I'd like to make a rabbit pie again."

It used to be the custom for lairds to tell their keepers to give a pair of rabbits at Christmas to all the estate workers. It was a very welcome present as they were often large families.

When I was still at school, I used to be adept at catching rabbits. I would get up at 6 a.m. and would go round my snares. Any rabbits were slung on the handlebars of my cycle — there were no school buses in those days — and delivered to a butcher in St Andrews before I went into school.

The price received was sixpence or, for a large one, ninepence. These "huge" amounts went into my savings.

I noticed in the butcher's shop recently that he was asking £2 for a rabbit — changed days.

"Are you kidding? I'd go out with him if he were my sister's *current* boyfriend."

Susan sighed theatrically. In fact, she and the buyer for Hobbies and Children's Books were moving at a sedate but certain pace towards an engagement.

"It was five years ago," Anne added.

"Practically pre-history," Susan said, and moved discreetly towards a group of youths clustered at the back of the store.

ALL the same, Ann decided to ring Val that night and see if the idea bothered her.

"Steve Anderson . . ." There was a long silence at the other end of the line, then Val asked, "Dark hair, about five-ten?"

"Blond hair and over six feet," Anne corrected her, with relief.

"Oh, Steve the Architect. He's nice," Val said. The conversation ended after a few amiable exchanges of news and gossip, and Anne looked forward to her evening out with a clear conscience.

Six weeks later, she was wondering if she'd made the right decision.

"I'm not even sure if he's interested in me," she confided to Susan during their coffee break.

"He's not taking you out every Saturday night because he hates you," Susan said in a practical tone. "All right, maybe you've fallen

by
John
Taylor

There were some rabbits in view, but too far away for my gun to have any effect. They scurried away as fast as their legs could carry them.

I got Anne two in the end, however. She jointed them, added onions and a thick gravy, plus a crust top with an egg cup in the middle of the pastry.

Home-grown potatoes were boiled and creamed and served with boiled cabbage fresh from her vegetable garden.

We enjoyed that meal thoroughly, and we talked about the time she made it regularly when the bairns were wee.

"We must do one again soon, dear," I said hopefully...

COMING back to Anne's two rabbits...
When I take the tractor or walk round the fields, particularly near the burn side, rabbits just sit and look at me or hop slowly to their burrows.

Nae bother, I thought, as I left the farm with my gun over my shoulder.

I think there must be a rabbit bush telegraph which lets them all know that the farmer with a gun has left the back door of the farmhouse.

harder than he has so far, but he must be interested."

"Oh, we always have a good time together. We have a lot of common interests, and we talk a lot. But that's pretty much it." In a quiet voice, Anne added, "He never looks at me in the dreamy way he used to look at Val."

"He's twenty-seven now, not twenty-two," Susan said kindly. "It makes a difference."

That night, Anne found it impossible to concentrate on the list of French irregular verbs she was meant to memorise for the next night's class. Instead she stared blankly at them, thinking, I have to find out before I get hurt.

First she rang her mother. Then she rang Steve.

In a careful, neutral tone, she said, "I'm going for the usual every-other-Sunday lunch with my family this weekend, and Mother wondered if you'd like to join us?"

"I'd love to," Steve replied promptly. "I have fond memories of your mother's cooking, and I think I could give your dad a better game of chess these days. And it will be interesting to see the *princesse lointaine* again."

What sort of princess? Anne reached for her French/English dictionary. "Lointaine" was translated as "distant." Ridiculous. Val wasn't the least bit distant. She was a warm, friendly girl.

After her French class the next night, she stayed behind to ask Mr

153

Sharpless, her teacher, if the words had a different meaning.

"It's a bit of a poetic term," he explained. "Think of a fairy tale princess in a tower or castle keep, whom the hero has to rescue by magic or bravery."

Fairy tale princess. Yes, Anne thought sadly, that fits.

IT was Anne who was distant, as Steve drove her out to her parents' house in the suburbs on Sunday.

"You're very quiet today," Steve commented. "Is anything the matter?"

"I suppose I feel a bit awkward about you and Val," Anne answered, wishing she were better at concealing her feelings.

Steve glanced briefly away from the wheel. "I should be the one feeling awkward, if anyone should be. It could be argued that I let Valerie down badly."

"What are you talking about?"

"Oh, you were probably too busy with your A Levels then to take much notice, but Val and I were definitely an item for a good while. I'm sure most people expected an engagement.

"I was thinking that way myself, for the first five or six months, until it started to hit me that unless we were actually doing something together — films, discos, tennis, whatever — we didn't have a lot in common."

Steve kept his eyes on the road, looking for the turn-off to her parents' street.

"You mean you were the one who broke it off?" Anne asked incredulously.

"'Fraid so. It should never have gone on as long as it did, but I was only twenty-two, and Val was so very lovely."

"Your fairy tale princess," Anne said in a low voice.

He nodded. "Complete with long, golden hair, just like the stories specify. As a child, you never stop to wonder what they do with the rest of their lives, that maybe staying in one place while she waits to be rescued may have given the princess a rather limited perspective on life."

"Val's not stupid or lazy," Anne said indignantly.

"No, she isn't, and I'm sorry if I sounded critical," he apologised. "I expected too much from her. The fault was mine."

And the rest of us expected too little. The thought popped unbidden into Anne's head, as they turned into the driveway of her parents' house.

Mr Cavendish ushered them into the living-room, and moments later Anne's mother came in to join them for a sherry. A faint, delicious aroma of roasting lamb followed her.

As Steve was explaining how he and Anne had met again in the bookshop, Val came down the short flight of stairs that led from her bedroom.

"Steve, it's good to see you again," she said in a warm, natural voice.

Anne stared at her sister in shock.

Her mother interpreted the look correctly, and commented, "I don't know what possessed Valerie to cut off all her beautiful hair, I really don't."

"For starters, it took two hours to dry every time I washed it." Val patted the blonde helmet of hair that was styled to just below her ears. "This takes ten minutes. What do you think, Annie?"

"It's so different . . ." She considered this new, trendy-looking version of her sister, and said firmly, "I like it."

OVER dinner, Steve did most of the talking, as her parents and Val pumped him for details of what he had been doing for the past five years.

He gave a slightly different summary of his ambitions than he had to Anne, saying, "Oddly enough, I'm no longer burning to design new buildings. I want to work with the interior space of existing houses, change them from dark and dull to light and exciting."

"Let me know when you've done your first conversion," Val said, as she passed Steve a plate of trifle. "I might be qualified to sell it for you by then."

"Valerie's enrolled in a course to become an estate agent herself," Mr Cavendish explained.

Anne's mother laughed in a disbelieving manner. "Can you imagine our Val as a businesswoman?"

"Yes, I can," Anne said, considering the idea.

As she had said to Steve, Val wasn't stupid or lazy. It was just that with everyone rushing to do things for her, there hadn't been much incentive for her to do anything for herself.

The two girls volunteered to do the washing-up.

As Anne dried, she said, "You knew perfectly well who Steve Anderson was when I phoned, didn't you?"

Val nodded. "I wasn't likely to forget the first man who dropped me, was I? A few years ago, I would have been furious, but now I realise we weren't remotely right for each other. I didn't want to put you off someone who might be very right for you."

Impulsively, Anne put her arm round Val's waist and gave her a hug. "I'm really glad you're doing this course. It's time you moved down from the tower."

Val stared at her blankly. "Tower? It's just a dormer bedroom."

As they were driving back to the city, Steve said, "That went very well, I thought, didn't you?"

"My parents always liked you, Steve. Or do you mean that the meal was good?"

"Your mother's excellent cooking is one of the few constants in a changing world," he replied. "But what I meant was that I'm pleased your parents can accept me in, shall we say, a new rôle?"

"Is that important to you?"

His hand left the steering wheel momentarily to cover hers and squeeze it. "Oh yes. It's important." □

looking out for Mary

I'LL never forget the first time I saw Aunt Mary in tears. She was staying with us temporarily, until she got married and moved into her cottage by the river.

Aunt Mary was, and still is, the happiest person I've ever known. She was always smiling and laughing. Mother used to shake her head and say that Aunt Mary would never grow up. I was glad — I didn't want her to change, ever.

I got a fright when I saw her cry that day, though. She usually came home from work about 5.30 p.m., and she'd sweep me into her arms, plant a million kisses on my cheeks, and tell me a joke or a funny story.

But she didn't that day. She crept in, her big brown eyes sad, and dropped her jacket on a chair.

My mother turned round to say something — she hated what she called "Mary's lazy ways" — but she took one look at the tear-stained face and closed her mouth again.

"Mary, love," she said with uncharacteristic tenderness, "whatever's happened?"

I saw Mary's chin wobble slightly as she flung herself down on the old wooden chair that was Mother's favourite.

"It's all off, Sheila." She sobbed, burying her face in her hands and slumping over the table.

That's all I heard at that point — Mother sent me next door to borrow some sugar from Mr Heggarty.

I was so upset over Mary's tears, that by the time I got next door I was almost crying too. Whatever could have happened to upset my favourite person? I'd no idea, but it had to be terrible.

AUNT Mary didn't go to work the next day. She spoke to Mother a lot, and more tears were shed. In the afternoon, she came to my room.

"Grab your coat and hat, pet," she said cheerily. "Let's go for a walk."

We went up to the moors at the back of our house. The wind whipped Mary's dark curls around her face, and she seemed to cheer up a bit, much to my relief.

We kicked through the autumn leaves, and she laughed when a bird flew out of the

by MARGARET GREENHILL

trees and made me jump.

When we got to the top, she flung herself down on the hard ground and stared at the scene below. I wasn't sure what to do about her sudden change of mood, so I wandered away to inspect a nearby rabbit burrow, knowing that if Mary wanted to talk to me, she would.

She called me over and pulled a sticky toffee from her pocket. That was something else I loved about Aunt Mary — she always had sweets with her, and she never, ever told Mother if I ate any.

She was my greatest childhood friend, and my biggest ally, too.

"I'm not getting married after all, Sally," she said sadly, gazing at the tapestry of fields below us. "He's met someone else . . ."

I flung myself into her arms. If Donald didn't want my beloved aunt, then he was surely blind or daft — or probably both. Anyone could see that she was the most beautiful person in the world, and good fun, too.

I have to admit that I was secretly relieved for a moment though, because I'd never liked Donald much. But when I saw the sadness in her face, I felt guilty.

We stayed on the hill for ages — until our fingers and toes began to feel numb, then made our way home.

Mother was frantic when we eventually turned up.

"Where have you been? You said an hour! I've been worried sick!"

"I'm sorry, Sheila." Mary didn't even have the strength to argue. I was beginning to worry about my favourite aunt.

Aunt Mary went back to work after that day, but the sparkle had gone from her eyes, and she didn't seem to know how to laugh any more.

She spent a lot of time on her own, and took long walks by herself along the river bank. She began to work a lot of overtime as well at the factory where she was a seamstress.

Mother and Father were worried about her too, I could tell.

"She's so pale and listless. I wish there was something I could do," I heard Mother tell Father when she thought I wasn't listening.

What Aunt Mary really needed was to be cheered up. I desperately wanted to do this, but didn't know how. She wasn't really interested in anything I had; I offered her my funniest comic, but she barely smiled, and I actually saw the tears well up when I offered her my favourite teddy bear to hold for a while.

A UTUMN moved into winter, and Mary still moped around with a long face. She made more of an effort at Christmas, but it didn't last long.

Mother lost her temper with Mary once, because she was so miserable, but luckily, the row didn't get too bad. Not even Mother could be angry with Mary for long.

As winter got colder, it began to snow. Mary smiled a lot when she saw it. We both loved the snow, and took great delight in making snowmen and having snowball fights.

It seemed like the old Mary was on the way back again, and although no-one said as much, we were all relieved.

I remember one particularly cold February day. It had snowed heavily, and Mary was working late again. Father decided to meet her from work and walk her home.

I pestered him until he gave in and let me go too. He sat me on his shoulders for some of the way, and we crunched happily through the thick snow.

I felt warm and cheerful, snuggled into my thick scarf. My gloves kept the cold out, and when Father let me down, I got a big snowball all ready for Mary when she left the factory.

I had to hide it from Father, though, just in case he wouldn't let me throw it.

At seven exactly, the door opened, and Mary came out, wrapped up in her thick coat. I launched my snowball quickly, and it flew across, knocking her hat off.

Her hair tumbled out and she let out a peal of laughter as she retaliated. We had a furious battle for a minute or so, until Father scooped me up on his shoulders again.

Just then, Mary let fly with another snowball. She missed us both, and gasped in horror as a complete stranger took her snowball full in the face.

She ran over to him.

"Are you all right? I'm terribly sorry . . ."

"So you should be!" spluttered the stranger, wiping snow from his spectacles which, fortunately, seemed undamaged. He put them back on and peered at Mary. "Aren't you a bit old to be acting so childishly?"

"I do hope you're not hurt," Mary said stiffly.

"I'm not, but I might have been. Take more care in future." The man looked sternly at Mary, and in the glow of the street lamp, I could see her turn a shade of pink.

The wind taken out of her sails, Mary picked up her hat, jammed it on her head, and we set off without another word.

I hoped that the snow would carry on all night, that we'd be snowed in, and Mary wouldn't be able to get to work the next day.

That had happened once before, and we had a wonderful day. Sadly, it was not to be. Mary went off to work as usual, and Mother got on with the household chores. The day passed quickly, because I got to help out.

That night, Mary looked quite different when she came home.

"Look what I've got!" She laughed, and dropped the biggest box of chocolates I'd ever seen on the table.

"They were handed in anonymously today — no card, no note, nothing. The boy from Bell's delivered them." She laughed again, and her eyes sparkled. "He said I had a secret admirer!"

Mother left the stove to take a look, and gasped when she saw the box.

"You certainly have!" She winked cheekily at Mary. "Bell's chocolates don't come cheap — and these must have cost a fortune!"

"I know." Mary blushed and smiled dreamily.

MARY was happier than she'd been for a while, that night. We even played Snap for a while. Then I sat on her knee in front of the fire, and she told me a story before I went to bed. She even gave me one of her chocolates — and it was lovely.

The next morning, I woke with the feeling that something exciting was going to happen. The snow was thawing, and I could hear a blackbird singing, perched on a tree in Mr Heggarty's garden.

When I went into the kitchen, Mother said that we'd have to take a trip into town — Mary had forgotten to take her lunch with her.

I was disappointed with the snow when we got outside — there wasn't enough left to make a snowball, never mind a snowman. I contented myself with skipping alongside Mother, jumping in the puddles whenever I thought she wasn't looking.

The place where Mary worked wasn't far away, and as we got nearer I saw a familiar figure leave and hurry off in the opposite direction.

It was the man that Mary had hit with the snowball that night! Perhaps he'd gone to shout at Mary again and make more trouble.

We went in to find Mary.

"You've brought my lunch!" She seemed taken aback. "Thank you very much, but you've come all this way for nothing.

"It was really kind of you and I do appreciate it, but I'm going out."

"The man with the snowball!" I cried excitedly, suddenly realising why he'd been there.

"That's right." Mary beamed. "His name's Johnny. He gave me the chocolates to apologise for being so bad tempered, but the card must have fallen off. He came to deliver it today — and then asked me out to lunch."

Aunt Mary was back to normal after that. I liked Johnny much more than Donald — he showed me how to skim stones in the river, *and* he knew lots of jokes.

Mary must have liked him too, because they got married the next spring. I was bridesmaid, and I had a lovely time, in spite of the fact that I had to wear a frilly dress.

In fact, it was one of the best days of my life, and I'll never forget it. Everyone laughed a lot, and danced all night. Mary positively glowed with happiness, and Johnny couldn't take his eyes off her.

★   ★   ★   ★

That all happened a long time ago — fifty years, to be exact, but nothing's changed.

My husband Andrew and I are delighted to be guests at Mary and Johnny's golden wedding party, and I'm sure I'm not the only one with a lump in my throat and tears in my eyes tonight.

The band are beginning the Anniversary Waltz, and as Johnny gently takes Mary's hand, I see her smile at him just like she did all those years ago.

Mary's still as sprightly as ever, still light on her feet and full of fun. Johnny's a dapper little man, with lovely now white hair and eyes that sparkle with merriment.

Tonight though, he only has eyes for Mary, and as we watch them circle the dance floor, they look just like those newly-weds all over again. □

WHAT A TEAM!

THANK goodness for the march of fashion, Tessa thought, zipping up her straight black skirt. Not long ago she'd have been reduced to safety-pins to keep her white blouse from riding up, but these newfangled bodies were a godsend. No matter what she did, she would stay smart for the occasion.

Reaching for her lipstick, she saw her hand reflected in the mirror. It was anything but steady. She was forty-six and usually had an air of calm composure.

This was worse than anything she'd ever known . . . except . . .

On her wedding day, a shy and nervous twenty, she had stood before another mirror in another bedroom, shivering

by HELEN MACKENZIE

with fright while fussing hands had slipped the yards of snowy satin into place.

It hadn't been until she'd actually caught a glimpse of Victor standing by the altar that her fears had been dispelled.

If only Victor could be here this minute! But he was busy in the office. She'd understood, of course.

"I'll be there for the ceremony," he had soothed at breakfast, when she'd abandoned all pretence of eating. "I've an important meeting, dear."

"You won't get too involved, though, and forget?"

"As if I could!" He laughed. "It's everyone's big day. You and Katy most of all. But me as well, in my small way."

"Not small." She reached out to touch his hand. "We'd neither of us have coped without all that support and love from you."

"I'll come and pick you up." He smiled. "Half past ten."

She was afraid of crumpling the skirt. Today would be the only day she'd ever wear it, but today it had to be exactly right, especially for Victor's photographs.

He was so proud that he had bought a whole new album for the purpose, which touched her deeply. Yet, on reflection, she decided it was she who should be proud of him. No husband could have possibly done more.

She'd had a job before they married, working in the local bank. Then bonnie, bouncing Joseph came along. So, ambitions deferred, she settled into motherhood, although it was a longer wait before the second baby.

Her thirties slipped away between loads of washing, heaps of ironing, the cooking and the washing up. She hardly had a moment free to brood upon what might have been, until her daughter started working for her first exams.

Then Tessa recollected how she'd slaved for hers. She thought of that certificate with all those GCEs. The waste!

"I wondered," she said hesitantly, "if I mightn't try for A-levels. There's quite a choice of adult classes at the Tech."

"Terrific!" Victor beamed. "I'm sure you'll do well."

At first it was astonishingly hard to discipline herself to study, never mind store things in her rusty memory, and run the house . . .

She muddled through from one day to another, never finding time

LOCH ARD, CENTRAL REGION

S ITUATED on the northern edge of the Queen Elizabeth Forest Park, Loch Ard is in the heart of the Trossachs, yet only an hour's travel from Glasgow. The thick woods in the area led to its name, which means "The Bristled Country." Made famous in Sir Walter Scott's "The Lady Of The Lake," the Trossachs is MacGregor country and was the scene of cattle rustling by Rob Roy MacGregor.

LOCH ARD, TROSSACHS : J CAMPBELL KERR

to lift her head and gaze at the horizon, until she passed with flying colours.

"You ought to try for university," Katy said, as she hugged her mother. "We could even go together."

"I'm far too old," she murmured deprecatingly.

"Rubbish!" Katy said.

"I've left it far too late."

"Better late than never." Victor sounded as if he actually believed that.

So Tessa's faded dreams of a career began to take on new colour.

"It's not as if I'd have to go away," she pointed out, more to persuade herself than Victor. "It's only half an hour's drive. The only problem is that I'd be studying full-time."

The penny dropped. Soon Victor had produced a detailed schedule, allocating chores around the house. He bore the greatest load.

"I'm settled in my job," he argued when she'd protested. "I've only got to trim my schedule and maybe delegate a bit. It certainly won't do me any harm."

He'd kept his word. He smoothed Tessa's passage through those three long years, and now he was about to see their teamwork crowned.

GLANCING at her watch, she saw it was a quarter to eleven, and still no sign of him. Across the landing, Katy's door was open.

"Snap!" She laughed as Tessa slipped into the room. "A real pair of penguins!"

"I only wish I had your figure for a blouse and skirt," said Tessa ruefully. "Still, I don't suppose much of me will show. I'll be a blur of shakes!"

Katy put her white-sleeved arm comfortingly around her mother.

"I bet everyone else is quaking in their shoes, and feeling pretty silly. Just when we reckoned we were out of school for ever, here we are in uniform again."

"Tradition, I suppose. And imagine what some people might wear for their graduation if there were no rules!"

Katy giggled.

"I see myself in silver lurex leggings and a scarlet body," she murmured, closing her eyes.

Tessa giggled, too, but then remembered Victor.

"You wouldn't ring the office? See if Dad's forgotten?"

"As if he would!"

"I'd ring myself, but I hate to seem a nag."

"All right, all right. I'll do it!" Katy said good humouredly, but she looked a little anxious as she put the phone back on the hook.

"Apparently, he went out half an hour ago to buy a roll of film."

"Honestly!"

"Better late than never!" Katy laughed.

"Perhaps we ought to take your car? It's getting awfully late."

"We haven't got to be there until quarter past," Katy protested.

"Even so," her mother said, "we can't take chances. Not today."

The room behind the hall was full of people poring over tables piled with academic gowns.

"Oh dear!" Tessa sighed. "I'd no idea it would be like this. I thought there'd be a little parcel with my name on it."

"It's more of a free-for-all," the girl beside her murmured. "Look at this! The fourth one that I've tried and absolutely useless. It's trailing on the floor."

Tessa smiled despite herself. The robe she had chosen barely reached her knees.

"Suppose we try a swap? I'm quite tall."

"Oh, perfect! For both of us."

She drifted off into the crowd, and Tessa scanned the heads in the hope of spotting Katy's auburn mop. Ah! There she was, admirably fitted out. Tessa moved towards her with a glow of pride. A daughter to be proud of.

"You're looking super!" Katy whispered in her ear. "A mother to be proud of!"

"But where's the father and the husband?"

Slipping off the bulky gown, Tessa peered out at the gathering audience.

"He isn't there," she whispered anxiously as Katy helped her back into the robe and led her to their place in the queue.

"Don't worry, Mum. Relax. Enjoy the moment."

Tessa found she couldn't *not* enjoy the moment, as the yellow hood belonging to her faculty was pinned in place, the mortar board placed delicately on her head, its tassel swinging to one side.

"You look terrific," Katy whispered.

"I feel terrific!" Tessa nodded and the tassel bobbed.

Music filled the auditorium. The dignitaries took their places on the stage behind the desk piled high with scrolls. It was an awe-inspiring moment, and Tessa was part of it.

She took a deep breath and held her shoulders back. Something in the way the heavy, deeply-pleated gown fell round her gave her suddenly a stately bearing. It was a marvellous sensation. All she needed now to make her happiness complete was Victor.

Wherever is he? she thought frantically, as she joined the line of students waiting for the presentation. Please, please not in a traffic jam! He mustn't miss this moment after all he's done towards it.

One by one the students started filing up the steps, across the stage then, scrolls received, they disappeared in the distance to the sound of loud applause. It was Katy now, and Tessa thrilled to see the slender figure of her daughter gliding through the ceremony.

A flash of light distracted Tessa's gaze. She stared, then smiled. There, in the last seat of the second row, sat Victor, camera in hand, his face aglow with haste and happiness.

Better late than never, she thought wryly as his flashlight blazed again, for her. □

TIM and Beth were going to spend Christmas on their own. Beth had mixed feelings. It was their first Christmas together since their marriage in August, and Beth had feared there would be problems.

"Oh, it's awful!" Anna in the office had groaned. "If we spend Christmas Day with my parents, I love it because we have the same traditions we've had since I was a kid — but Mike thinks it's very quiet, with just the four of us.

"Then we have to skedaddle across town to spend Boxing Day with Mike's mum and dad and what seems like forty other relatives — which I hate. Or, we do it in reverse — and that's even worse! Mike's parents don't open any presents 'til the evening and they never eat until about nine and — "

The cry had been taken up all round the office. Beth had sighed. Splitting yourself in two seemed to cause no end of problems over the festive season — and no-one seemed to enjoy it.

She so wanted this first Christmas with Tim to be memorable and happy. It would be the first in their little house, the first as Mrs Walker.

But — and there was a but — she had a pang of regret when she thought about all the previous happy Christmases she'd spent at home with her parents.

She and Tim had talked about it, of course, and come up with the same idea as Anna — Christmas Day with Beth's parents, Boxing Day with Tim's. It wouldn't be ideal for either of them, but what other solution was there?

Their parents, unexpectedly, answered the question for them.

"We're going away for Christmas," Beth's mum had said in November. "Dad and I have booked a little hotel in the country. I've been cooking Christmas dinner for nearly thirty years — I thought it would be nice to let someone else do the work.

"Anyway — " she'd smiled at Beth over her coffee cup " — I'm sure you and Tim will want to spend your first Christmas together, won't you? So it'll be pointless for Dad and me to have a turkey and all the trimmings on our own. I'm looking forward to being spoiled . . ."

Beth had smiled back and said she hoped her parents had a smashing time — and felt a little sad over the ending of a tradition.

by CHRISTINA JONES

A PROPER Christmas

She also thought, with a sinking heart, that this would leave Christmas Day open to spend with her in-laws.

Much as she loved Tim's family, she didn't want to be like Anna and the other girls in the office, and have to fit in with a strange routine, not at Christmas. But how could she tell Tim without hurting his feelings?

Again, she didn't have to.

"We're off to Rosie's for the whole of Christmas," Mrs Walker informed them cheerfully. Rosie was Tim's sister who had just had her second baby. "She's so busy with the two little ones, I thought it was the least we could do. And you two can have a proper Christmas, here, in your own home, can't you?"

IT had all been arranged, and Beth and Tim had chosen decorations and a real tree — both their families had artificial ones — and had tramped the hills in a biting wind looking for holly and mistletoe and strands of dark, glossy ivy.

They'd discussed it all between hugs and kisses. The little house — beautiful in its traditional décor — rang with laughter. They'd go to the midnight service, they'd have stockings which they'd open as soon as they woke up, they'd open the main presents under the tree after breakfast, they'd both prepare the meal — which was to be eaten at midday.

They'd walk it off across the hills before curling in front of the television with a drink and all the delicious Christmas bits and pieces that they had been buying on their regular, weekly supermarket trip.

Beth sighed happily. It was going to be perfect.

Christmas morning dawned dark and blustery, with the clouds low and yellow across the hills. Beth shivered in her dressing-gown and turned up the heating.

They'd opened their stockings and laughed over the silly presents they had chosen for each other, and after breakfast, they'd kissed under the mistletoe in the tiny hall.

Beth was speechless at the beauty of the bracelet Tim had bought her, and Tim had picked her up and whirled her round the room when he'd opened his camera. There wasn't much money left after paying the mortgage, but they'd managed.

"Do you miss your family?" Beth asked, as they peeled a mountain of sprouts in the shoe-box kitchen.

"We're our family, now." Tim leaned over and kissed the tip of her nose. "It's different, of course, but I'm very happy. What about you?"

"I miss them a bit," Beth admitted, starting on the potatoes and passing the carrots to Tim, "but I bet none of them are enjoying it as much as we are. Don't you think we've done far too many vegetables?"

Tim peered into the saucepans and nodded.

"Definitely — still, we can have bubble and squeak for the rest of the week, can't we? And the turkey will last until Easter!"

A Proper Christmas

BETH hurried into the dining-room to arrange crackers on the table. It was freezing.

She turned the heating up and touched the radiators. They were stone-cold.

Worriedly, she hurried back to the kitćen.

"Tim, I think there's something wrong with the heating . . ."

Tim hurried off to check the boiler, and the phone rang. It was her parents calling from the hotel.

"Happy Christmas to you both!" Her mother sounded very happy. "This is a wonderful place — all I have to do is nothing! I could get used to this way of life. It's lovely to have a rest — and Dad sends his greetings."

Beth's mother chatted for a bit longer, and by the time Beth put the receiver down, her feet were numb.

"Dead as a doornail." Tim's face was solemn. "I think we'll just have to put on extra sweaters. There's no-one we can call out today!"

"We've got our love to keep us warm," Beth quoted with a grin, pushing her feet into her old furry slippers, just as the first snowflakes started to fall.

Tim's parents phoned from Rosie's. There were screams of excitement from the children, and Tim's mum sounded delighted to be organising a big family Christmas with youngsters around to enjoy it.

When Beth put the phone down her nose was icy.

She ran to the window and watched the fat, goosefeather flakes drifting across the hills. It was so beautiful. The grey-brown gardens were already wearing a cloak of transparent white, and the sky promised more snow to come.

"I'm going to have a word with Mr Maynard," Tim said after they'd checked that the turkey was spitting succulently in the oven and they were both wearing three sweaters. "Maybe he'll know about the boiler. They're probably all the same in these houses."

Mr Maynard lived next door and had been very helpful ever since they'd moved in, lending them ratchet screwdrivers and drills and all manner of intricate tools that neither of them recognised but would have been lost without.

Tim pulled his leather jacket over his sweaters, and shuddered as he stepped out into the icy blast.

Mr Maynard's house was even colder than theirs.

"Never bothered with central heating," he told Tim. "We never had it in my day. You youngsters are cosseted! Since Elsie died I've lived more or less in one room. Still, I'll come and have a look for you. Just let me get my coat . . ."

Tim looked round the room. There were no decorations, no tempting fragrance of Christmas dinner, only half a dozen Christmas cards on the mantelpiece. Tim thought of the happiness of his own little house next door, and counted his blessings.

"It's the pump, I'm afraid." Mr Maynard emerged from under the boiler ten minutes later, shaking his head. "Unless you've got one of those twenty-four-hour service call-out things, I think you'll have to do without it 'til after the holidays."

Beth and Tim looked at each other. They hadn't been able to afford a service agreement. It was one of the things they'd planned for next year when their budget wasn't quite so tight.

"Sorry I can't help you." Mr Maynard gazed at the streamers and the holly and ivy and the big bunch of mistletoe. "I hope it doesn't spoil your Christmas."

He grinned. "You'll have to snuggle up together — just like Elsie and I did when we were first married."

Tim looked at Beth again, then grinned back at Mr Maynard.

"Please stay for dinner," he urged.

"I couldn't possibly — I couldn't interfere — I mean, you youngsters want to be on your own and — "

Beth had interpreted Tim's eye signals, and touched Mr Maynard's arm.

"Have you got a Christmas dinner waiting? Are you expecting anyone?"

"Well, no," the old man admitted. "We didn't have any children, Elsie and me, and there's no family left. I don't do much over Christmas these days, except . . ."

Beth smiled at him.

"Except? Oh, please stay, Mr Maynard. No-one should be on their own at Christmas. And we've got loads and loads of food!" She giggled. "This being our first one we've overdone everything! We could feed the street!"

Mr Maynard sniffed appreciatively. How many years had it been since Christmas morning had smelled like this?

He looked at his young neighbours and saw himself and Elsie fifty years ago when they'd first moved to the terrace. They'd been completely broke and ecstatically happy, just like Tim and Beth.

"If you're sure I'm not going to be in the way . . ."

"Definitely not!" Tim ushered him into the living-room. "What would you like to drink?"

"Mr Maynard — " Beth called as she warmed her hands on the

PITTENWEEM, FIFE

*T*HE name means "place of the cave." Pittenween has been a royal burgh since 1541. It is a picturesque place with crow-stepped gables indicating a once-thriving trade with the Netherlands, France and Scandinavia. Today its busy harbour is usually crowded with fishing boats.

PITTENWEEM, FIFE : J CAMPBELL KERR

cooker " — you said just now you didn't do anything except — and you didn't finish it."

"Oh, I usually go down to Mrs Greenwood at Fifty-Seven for the Queen's Speech. It's become a bit of a tradition. She's on her own, too. I'll pop down and explain."

"No." Beth shook her head. "Stay here and have a drink with Tim. I'll go."

T HE snow was gusting in stinging clouds as Beth hurried, slipping and sliding, along the street. Although it was freezing, it was so beautiful, so in keeping with the day, that her heart soared.

She liked Mrs Greenwood. The old lady always stopped for a chat and had given her lots of tips about the garden. Beth knocked on the door.

Mrs Greenwood didn't have any decorations either. She had quite a lot of cards — a huge one from her only son and his family in Canada — and was sitting by one bar of her electric fire.

Beth explained the situation, then smiled winningly.

"So, if you just get your coat," she began.

"What? No, dear. I couldn't, I just couldn't. It's very kind of you but — "

But Beth would accept no excuses.

"As long as you don't mind being cold because of the boiler," Beth went on.

Mrs Greenwood nodded ruefully towards the electric fire.

"That's the only bit of heat I can afford, my dear. I'm used to being not very warm, but I can't come to you just for my dinner."

"No, you can't." Beth lifted up a coat and headscarf. "You can have tea and supper and the Queen's Speech as well. We might not have any heat but we've tons of everything else!"

Like love, she thought happily, as Mrs Greenwood pulled on her coat, and happiness. Those two alone were worth more than all the riches in the world.

By the time they got back, Mr Maynard was telling Tim that the fireplace wasn't blocked off, just boarded over. If they didn't mind the risk of a soot fall, he'd fetch some logs and try to start a fire.

"That'd be wonderful." Beth's eyes shone as she poured Mrs Greenwood a sherry. "Come on, let's leave the men to the dirty work. We'll go and sit in the kitchen — it's warmer there."

Mrs Greenwood looked at the twinkling tree, the brightly-coloured decorations and the discarded wrapping paper in the corner. She thought of her family so far away in Canada, then at Beth's pretty, excited face. Just how she'd been, that first Christmas with her Fred . . .

There was no soot fall, and Mr Maynard proved to be a wizard with fires. The logs were crackling and spitting, and orange and blue flames leapt comfortingly up the chimney. The house was growing warmer by the minute.

Parting

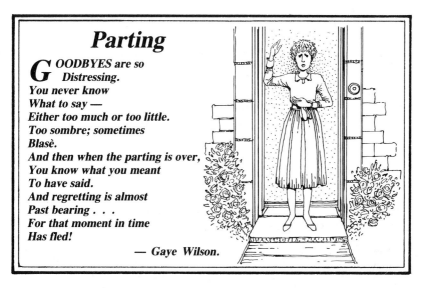

G OODBYES are so
Distressing.
You never know
What to say —
Either too much or too little.
Too sombre; sometimes
Blasè.
And then when the parting is over,
You know what you meant
To have said.
And regretting is almost
Past bearing . . .
For that moment in time
Has fled!

— Gaye Wilson.

B ETH and Tim pulled the dining-table into the living-room, and
Mrs Greenwood bustled round polishing glasses, laying out
plates and checking the sprouts.

The snow hissed and rattled against the windows. The fire roared
in the grate. It was deliciously cosy.

They sat and watched the Queen's Speech, none of them able to
move after what they all said had been the best Christmas dinner
ever.

Beth glowed with pride. She snuggled against Tim on the sofa and
felt his comforting arm round her shoulders.

"The first of many," he whispered. "I love you."

"I love you, too." She kissed his cheek.

They looked at Mr Maynard and Mrs Greenwood, sitting on either
side of the fire, heads nodding drowsily under their paper hats,
exhausted by their reminiscences of Christmas past, snug, warm and
happy.

Tim cuddled Beth even tighter as the snow whipped into a blizzard
in the rapidly fading light and the fire cast dancing shadows across
the ceiling.

"You know what we're having, don't you?" He smiled gently in the
warm glow.

"No," Beth murmured sleepily. "Tell me."

"We're having a proper Christmas."

Beth opened her eyes and looked at her husband in delight.

"Yes, we are, aren't we? A proper Christmas . . ." □

Printed and Published in Great Britain by D. C. Thomson & Co., Ltd., Dundee, Glasgow and
London. © D. C. Thomson & Co., Ltd., 1997. While every reasonable care will be taken, neither
D. C. Thomson & Co., Ltd., nor its agents will accept liability for loss or damage to colour
transparencies or any other material submitted to this publication.

ISBN 0-85116-624-5
EAN 9-780851 166247